A Candlelight Ecstasy Romance®

"YOU CAME HERE WITH THIS WHOLE THING PREMEDITATED," JACK SAID.

"You tricked me into doing your portrait, and then you planned how to draw me into your web, just like a spider!" He waved his arms about as he spoke. "And me, the unsuspecting fly, fell closer until I got caught in your trap!"

Marla could almost laugh if she weren't so outraged. "How did I seduce you? All I did was sit on this couch. You didn't have to come over here and rip apart my blouse! That was all your idea, Mr. Smug and Self-Righteous!" So what if she had planned the whole thing? It wasn't her fault he had cooperated so easily!

CANDLELIGHT ECSTASY ROMANCES®

THE
TEMPTRESS
TOUCH

Lori Herter

A CANDLELIGHT ECSTASY ROMANCE®

Published by
Dell Publishing Co., Inc.
1 Dag Hammarskjold Plaza
New York, New York 10017

Dell ® TM 681510, Dell Publishing Co., Inc.

Candlelight Ecstasy Romance®, 1,203,540, is a registered
trademark of Dell Publishing Co., Inc., New York, New York.

ISBN: 0-440-18568-8

Printed in the United States of America

First printing—September 1985

To Our Readers:

We have been delighted with your enthusiastic response to Candlelight Ecstasy Romances®, and we thank you for the interest you have shown in this exciting series.

In the upcoming months we will continue to present the distinctive sensuous love stories you have come to expect only from Ecstasy. We look forward to bringing you many more books from your favorite authors and also, the very finest work from new authors of contemporary romantic fiction.

As always, we are striving to present the unique, absorbing love stories that you enjoy most—books that are more than ordinary romance. Your suggestions and comments are always welcome. Please write to us at the address below.

Sincerely,

The Editors
Candlelight Romances
1 Dag Hammarskjold Plaza
New York, N.Y. 10017

CHAPTER ONE

So, here we are again, Marla thought as she sat down on the comfortable easy chair. *Same house, same room, same people —minus one: Jack.*

They had just finished dinner. Ginger and Devin had invited her to sit in the living room, refusing her offer to help them clear the dishes. She could hear light clinking noises from the table as she sat facing the fire. So far the evening had been pleasant, even fun.

It had been six weeks since she'd last been to this house on Double Bluff Beach, the house she had sold to Devin. When she drove up earlier, just seeing the quaintly styled wood structure was an unpleasant reminder of all that had happened here. But the cordial company of Ginger and Devin MacPherson made her forget it all for a time as they sat around the colonial dining room table enjoying Ginger's good cooking. The house looked warm and delightful now that Ginger had decorated it with her own personal touch.

Marla's thougtful dark eyes glanced away from the waning fire in the large fireplace and out the picture window toward the bay. It was early autumn, and the sky was already growing dark. The setting sun made shimmering patterns on the calm waters of shallow Useless Bay. The name made her chuckle softly to herself. So many places on Whidbey Island had colorful names—Cranberry Lake, Deception Pass, Saratoga Passage. No wonder it had been easy for her to be successful as a real estate agent on this romantic, crooked island in Puget Sound. She was glad she had made the move here several years ago from nearby Seattle, where she had grown up.

"Would you like an after-dinner drink, Marla?" Devin asked, coming from the kitchen.

"Yes, thanks. Crème de menthe?" she said, crossing her slender legs and pulling her straight skirt over her knee.

"Sure!" Devin said. After looking in a couple of cabinets he went back into the kitchen. Marla couldn't help but smile as she heard him say, "Ginger, where are the liqueur glasses?"

Together they were an adorable couple: blond, pretty, high-strung Ginger, and Devin, the man Ginger had loved all her life. Marla was glad everything had worked out for them, that they were happily remarried after so many years apart. After that night here six weeks ago, it hadn't looked like anything would ever be right again for any of them.

Marla felt as if a weight were settling on her slim shoulders: guilt. Would things ever be straightened out between her and Jack? Would he ever even be civil to her again? Even now she could still recall every word they had shouted at each other in this very room.

"I don't owe you any explanations!" Marla had said to Jack that night six weeks ago. Devin was silently watching them argue. "We've just been sitting here talking and having coffee," she said. "What excuse do *you* have for pounding the door down like that?"

"I had reason to believe there was more going on between you two than just talk," Jack said, his tall frame looming over her though she was tall herself. She remembered his blond hair falling onto his forehead as he gestured sharply—he always talked with his hands—and his blue eyes blazing with anger. "I won't embarrass you with some of the things Ginger told me. I just want to make it clear I'm not going to put up with this anymore!"

"I'm not going to put up with *you* trying to keep me on a

10

leash!" Marla retorted. "If I can't even spend an evening talking with a friend who happens to be male . . ."

"What were you talking about?" Jack asked, folding his arms over his chest as if daring her to make some reasonable explanation. "Interest rates?"

"We were talking about Ginger! Not that it's any of your business! I'm her best friend, and Devin has often asked me for advice about some of their problems."

Jack turned on Devin then. It was an unusual scene: two handsome, educated, ordinarily good-natured men glowering at each other. "So you just invited her over for some coffee, since Ginger was supposed to be away for the evening?" Jack said, his eyes like red coals. "Is that how it was?"

Devin answered with tethered patience. "Marla called about seven and asked if I'd be home so she could bring over a housewarming gift from her real estate agency. When she got here, I offered her some coffee and we got to talking. I've been having problems with Ginger and . . ."

"I see," Jack said more quietly, apparently believing Devin.

"And what prompted you to come here like this?" Marla asked Jack angrily. She should have known better than to ask. She should never have been so open and frank with Ginger in the first place.

"Ginger saw that your car has been in Devin's driveway all evening," Jack told Marla. "I happened to call her, after she went back home, to ask if she knew where you were. I was stupid enough to have gotten worried about you. She told me, and together we assumed the worst. But from what you'd told her in the past, Marla, I'd say the assumption wasn't out of line!"

At that point Ginger made her presence known; she had driven out to the house with Jack and was listening from the kitchen. A second argument erupted then between Devin and Ginger.

11

The echoes of all the shouting were still in Marla's ear when Devin said, "Here's your crème de menthe." His tone was easy and cordial, and it brought Marla back to the quiet of the present.

"Thanks," she said with a smile. She took the small stemmed glass from him.

"Ginger will be done in a minute," he said and walked to the fireplace. Marla watched as he added another log while she sipped her drink. Devin was handsome, all right. He had more of the perfection of a Greek statue than Jack did, who was taller but thinner and . . . well, not quite so neat. Jack was an artist who always seemed to have traces of paint on his shirt cuffs. Devin looked like he was born in a gray three-piece suit. Even now, in a white pullover sweater, he looked casually classic. As always, his brown hair was perfectly groomed, his thin tortoiseshell glasses giving him that precise, reliable look a CPA ought to have. Devin was also a few years younger than Jack. At thirty-eight, Jack's face showed his experience and perhaps a touch of world-weariness in spite of his aura of energy and joie de vivre.

Yes, Devin was handsome and bright, but after knowing Jack, she should have sensed that Devin wasn't the man for her. But she had been so mixed up back then, confused about her feelings for Jack, who all at once seemed to have set his mind on turning their brief affair into a marriage.

"How's Jack? Have you seen him lately?" Devin asked conversationally as he sat opposite her on the green-and-beige plaid couch.

Marla self-consciously ran her fingers through her long, thick, brunet hair. "No . . . not really." She still found herself slightly embarrassed around Devin when the subject of her breakup with Jack arose. Her brief interest in Devin had been the cause of her split with Jack. She could speak of the matter freely with Ginger; in fact she did, often, when they met for lunch. But Devin was still blissfully unaware.

"He still doesn't want to try to patch things up?" Devin asked.

"No," Marla said with a quiet sigh.

Devin shook his head. "I'm surprised. I thought Jack was more reasonable. He knows now there was nothing going on between you and me. I don't know why he would have thought there was. Why is he still upset with you?"

Marla shrugged uneasily. "I'm—too independent for him," she said. In a way it was true, and it was the most innocent answer she could think of. She wished she had actually been so innocent in the matter. Devin still didn't have a full understanding of what had been going on around him back then. Ginger apparently had decided not to enlighten him, either. Marla couldn't blame her. Why should Ginger tell her husband her best friend had been chasing him?

Ginger came in now. She sat down on the couch next to Devin, curling up in the crook of his protective, encircling arm. God, they were in love! It was only a little over a month ago that they had remarried each other. Seeing them now, it was hard to believe Ginger had once insisted she would never take Devin back again.

They were childhood sweethearts who had married young. Very soon after the first wedding, Ginger found out about a quick, meaningless affair Devin had gotten involved in while they were engaged. Hurt and feeling betrayed, Ginger had quickly divorced him. Devin left the area altogether then, but after years of loneliness and regret, he returned to try to win her back. With time and a great deal of patience he finally succeeded, but not without getting an ulcer from Ginger's constant rebuffs.

Marla had known Ginger still loved Devin and thought the couple ought to be reunited. But for a while, even though she was involved with Jack at the time, Marla had also felt attracted to Devin herself. When Marla had taunted Ginger one day, saying *she* would be happy to take Devin if Ginger didn't want him, Ginger had said, "Be my guest!" Having gotten permission, so to speak, Marla did make a few mild attempts to catch Devin's interest. But Devin was totally oblivious to all her signals; his eyes, mind and heart were set on Ginger alone.

In fact, it had been a little deflating. Marla was used to getting men's attention easily. Sometimes she got it without even trying, often attracting men she wished she hadn't. Her long legs, slim svelte figure, luxurious hair and dark coloring had always turned men's heads since she was a teenager. But to Devin, she was merely the real estate agent who had sold him the house he wanted at Double Bluff and, coincidentally, the best friend of the woman he loved so dearly.

"You're not too independent for Jack," Ginger said, picking up on Marla's lame explanation. "You're perfect for him!"

Marla smiled, the trace of sadness in her eyes replaced by a hint of the playfulness that was more typical of her. "Well, we all know *that's* true, but Jack hasn't caught on yet."

"What do you mean? He asked you to marry him, didn't he?" Devin said.

Marla sighed, and her expression showed her chagrin. "Yes, he did. And I treated it like a joke! He was so serious, it scared me off, I guess. I was used to my no-strings lifestyle and afraid of what I was feeling for him. I didn't quite realize I had . . ." She was going to say *fallen in love with Jack,* but somehow couldn't. She wasn't used to discussing her deepest feelings. "I didn't even think I was an emotional sort of person," she said instead.

She smiled, but felt her lips trembling slightly. This wouldn't do. Pushing herself back into the seat, she straightened. "But I've made up my mind," she said, sounding more determined. "I'm going to marry him."

Ginger's round eyes widened. "But—he's been so adamant about not wanting to see you."

"Well, he'll just have to change his attitude, that's all."

"How will you manage it?" Ginger asked.

"Simple," Marla said, putting confidence in her voice. "I have a plan."

Late that evening Marla drove back to her small house located just outside the tiny business area of Langley, a town on the other side of the narrow island. As she pulled into the gravel driveway, her headlights caught a flash of white fur and a plumed tail racing away into the darkness from the vicinity of her garbage can. So it was a cat that had been making all that racket the night before.

She got out of the car, unlocked her front door and went in. The lights were already on, as she had left them. She never used to worry about living alone or coming home by herself at night, but lately, for some reason, she did. She was probably just getting wiser as she got older, she thought. Soon she'd be thirty. The adolescent outlook that nothing could happen to her was finally disappearing. On the other hand, maybe she had just been around her worry-wart friend Ginger too long. She shouldn't knock it, she told herself. Careful, cautious Ginger was living happily with the man she adored, while carefree Marla was alone and miserable.

She slipped off her jacket and hung it in the closet off her living room, then plopped down on her white, modern-style couch. Across the room was her stone fireplace with the charred remnants of a log still lying in it. Above was a large painting, the seascape Jack had painted, a brilliant mixture of sun and stormclouds over a choppy sea, the waves sending spray over treacherous rocks in the foreground.

That painting had been her introduction to him. Several months ago she had decided she needed a painting to hang over her fireplace. One day she walked into his art gallery and bought that one. Actually it wasn't the first time she'd met him. They had seen each other around town now and then since he'd moved to Langley over two years before. But it was the first time she'd really talked to him and gotten to know him a little.

15

Frankly, at first she hadn't been all that impressed. He was lanky, thin, a little loose-jointed in the way he moved. His blond hair had hints of gray, though his eyes were blue enough. His mustache was a little overgrown. She remembered she'd had the urge to offer to trim it for him.

The thing that had struck her the most was that he talked so much. The initial thought she'd had was that he was nervous and trying to impress her. But he kept it up all through their dinner together at a restaurant that evening, and she began to think it was his natural way. Discussing it the next day at lunch with Ginger, who knew him well, confirmed it. Apparently he'd always talked a lot, sometimes about painting or his art gallery, but mainly about other people he knew, most of whom seemed to be women.

Marla had thought him amusing, something of a character. That was why the events of her second date with him were quite unexpected. She didn't know why she had slept with him so easily. It had started out with a few innocent kisses, and then. . . .

Well, there was no use playing that through her mind again. She'd just spend another sleepless night remembering better times, missing him. It was late and she had important plans for tomorrow. She'd better go to bed and try to sleep.

A half hour later she was just dozing off in bed in the darkened house when a sudden clatter woke her. It came from the back. Once her heartbeat had calmed a bit, she decided it sounded like the lid of her garbage can falling onto the gravel driveway. The darn cat had come back again.

She slipped on her quilted robe and went into the kitchen. Looking out the back window, in the moonlight she could see a patch of white moving across the lawn back toward the garbage can. Apparently the sudden clamor had briefly frightened the cat, too.

When she began to open the back door with the intention of going out and chasing the animal away, it suddenly turned and ran. *Well! If it's that skittish it shouldn't mess with people's garbage!* she thought irritably. She hurried out into the cold night air to put the lid back on the can. Shivering, she went back into the house.

Dumb cat! she thought as she opened the refrigerator and took out a quart of milk. She poured herself a glassful, hoping it would help her get back to sleep. As she was finishing the milk, she happened to glance out the window. The patch of white was cautiously creeping toward the garbage again. With a sigh she opened the refrigerator and took out a small container of leftover tuna casserole she'd made last night.

When she opened the door to put the food out, the cat ran again. "Kitty. Here, kitty, kitty, kitty." She saw the glow of two round eyes as the cat paused to look back; then it ran even faster toward the rear of her lot. In an instant it had disappeared behind some bushes.

"Gee, am I so frightening?" Marla asked herself. It reminded her of her dealings with Jack lately. She set the container of food on the outside doorstep, in case the cat should return, and went back in.

As she got into bed again, she remembered that her home cooking had also failed to entice Jack. A week after their falling out, she had invited Jack over for dinner, hoping they could talk things over, but he had refused to come. Later he declined her invitation to have lunch with her the following week, saying he was too busy. She even proposed having breakfast at a local restaurant before work one day, but he found some excuse. Finally, when she called him one afternoon from her office and suggested they have coffee together, he said he didn't drink coffee anymore. Whenever she dropped in at his gallery, he was always busy with a customer or he suddenly had an important phone call to make.

Marla sighed again as she stared into the darkness. Well, tomorrow was another day. She'd better have some luck with her new approach. She was running low on ideas.

17

A few long blocks away, Jack Whiting was finishing the background of the commissioned portrait of a Seattle businessman. His eyes were tired from working under the strong artificial lights that hung from the ceiling in the room that served as his studio. He preferred to work under the natural light of day, but he wanted to get this painting finished.

It wasn't that he was behind schedule. He would be finished with the painting well before it was expected. But working late into the night kept his mind focused, so it wouldn't stray to subjects he preferred not to dwell on. And wearing himself out helped him to sleep.

But sometimes when he worked too long his mind played tricks on him. Instead of the face he was painting he would begin to see beguiling shadowy eyes, billowing dark hair, red lips beckoning softly. . . .

He tossed the brush down on the table to his right, which held a colorful mess of half-squeezed tubes of paints, rags, brushes, an old jar of turpentine. When would he ever get Marla out of his head? he asked himself. Marla Rosetti. He wished he'd never met her. Beautiful and callous, exciting and fickle, she'd come into his life like fireworks. Suddenly he'd been alive, could feel feelings as intense as he'd ever had when engulfed in work on a painting; suddenly he'd joined the real world, had fallen in love with a real person.

If he was going to fall for someone after all these years, why did it have to be her? he wondered as he began to clean his brushes with the rags and turpentine. Why couldn't it have been someone steady, a woman who wasn't so set on being independent, someone he could trust? He must have been like a toy to her, a diversion. Maybe she'd never been with an artist before, he thought bitterly.

He shouldn't have let himself get so involved with her so quickly. *Let's face it, you let her seduce you!* he told himself. He had stupidly thought she was as on fire for him as he was for her. But she had always kept him on the periphery of her life, while he had wanted her in the center of his. He could still hear her laughter when he had suggested marriage. He should have known then she wasn't worthy of his love. But no, he stuck it out, hoping her attitude would change, only to find out she'd been chasing Devin MacPherson all along!

He threw the rag down, angry at Marla, angry at himself for rehashing it all once again. Well, he had learned his lesson: Don't get so involved with a woman until you know what her true character is. If he had restrained himself, allowed time to get to know her, he would have found out she was manipulative, uncaring and much too easy with men.

Or would he have? *Come on, let's be honest,* he told himself. *You couldn't have resisted her. You barely can now, even knowing what she is.*

Just thinking of her sometimes set his blood boiling. All his life he'd had an extremely vivid imagination. It came from being an only child who had had to entertain himself most of the time. He had long ago learned to channel the striking visions his mind could create to his canvases, transferring that kaleidoscopic energy into his paintings. But since Marla entered his life, most of his imaginings had become centered on her. Sometimes his memories and mental visions of Marla were so strong they gave him a feeling of her presence almost as real as if she were with him. But his strong emotions no longer had anywhere to express themselves now that he had pushed her out of his life.

He glanced back at the portrait on the easel before turning out the lights. *Maybe I should paint her,* he thought. He knew he could do it from memory. Since the first time he'd seen her in town, long before he became involved with her, he'd wanted to do a portrait of her. Her features were unusual and exquisite. When he was with her he'd often studied them, and he knew every detail of her face and form by heart.

But would painting her, putting her likeness on canvas, take her out of his mind once and for all? Or would the portrait of her become a new obsession, an icon for him to mourn over?

He rubbed his eyes with his fingertips. It was late, he was tired, and he was beginning to think crazy thoughts. His emotional life had been so stable before. What had that woman done to him?

He had to go home and get some sleep. Tomorrow was Monday, and he'd have to be up early to open the gallery. Monday. Marla's day off. What would she be doing? He hadn't seen her for nearly two weeks. Had she finally stopped pestering him? Had she found someone new?

CHAPTER TWO

"You think you can just say you're sorry and everything will be forgotten?"

"Can't we at least discuss it?"

"Discuss it! Your behavior isn't worth discussing!"

So went their final argument after Jack had found Marla at Devin's house that night. The words kept hammering through her head as Marla walked downhill along Anthes Avenue toward First Street, which bordered the waterfront. She had tried to apologize to Jack that night after they left Double Bluff. She had admitted it was wrong of her to try to attract the interest of another man when she was involved with Jack. But the apology did not pacify Jack in the least.

Marla's sense of guilt had prevented her from dealing with the situation calmly, as she usually would have done. She and Jack had wound up speaking bitterly to each other. When she had asked, "Can't we even be friends?" he had said, "All I know is we'll never be lovers again! I don't make the same mistake twice!" He had been avoiding her ever since.

Not anymore! Marla decided. She would be a woman who would not be ignored. And any future arguments with Jack would be handled much better than she had dealt with their last one, she vowed.

She turned left onto First Street near Langley's historic old totem pole. Steps nearby led down to the beach and the waters of Saratoga Passage. Marla began tucking her blouse into the waistband of her calf-length full skirt. The white blouse was rather Victorian-looking, with a high collar, lace and long leg-of-mutton sleeves. She had chosen it on purpose that morning. Jack treated her lately as if she were some sort of tramp, and the blouse had been selected to make her look as sweet and old-fashioned as possible. Her long dark hair was fastened back from her face with barrettes, giving her a somewhat innocent look. But just to keep her from looking too frail, she'd worn her knee-high leather boots below the ruffled blue skirt.

Her pace slowed as she came to an old wood-frame house, newly painted yellow. A hand-painted sign hung from the roof of the small porch and said JOHN R. WHITING ART GALLERY. *Here we go,* Marla thought, mentally bracing herself for rejection.

Inside, Jack was in a large first-floor room of the made-over two-story house, hanging three new paintings a Seattle artist had just delivered to him on consignment. In addition to his own works, his gallery also displayed paintings by various other Washington artists. With the growing tourist trade from the mainland, his gallery was increasingly successful and was lately keeping him busier than he liked to be.

He heard the bells on his front door jingle. After gently setting the painting he was handling against the wall, he walked into the front room to greet his customer.

His heart felt as if it had stopped for a moment when he saw her standing there, the white of her blouse radiant from the bright sunlight coming through the large front windows. It contrasted wonderfully with her olive skin and dark hair. She was a vision.

Jack had to hide a mixture of feelings as he gazed at Marla. He felt a sense of sheer, foolish joy just to be able to look at her again. But he also felt anger and impatience tightening his facial and neck muscles. Marla, here again? Would she never leave him alone? Didn't she know where she wasn't wanted? But there was another feeling deep within him he would never admit: relief.

"Hello, Jack," she said. Her voice was always soft and easy, at odds with her straightforward manner.

"Hello," he said coolly.

"It's been almost two weeks since we've seen each other."

"It has?"

"Yes!" she said, showing her most dazzling smile.

"Couldn't have been. It was just the other day I told you I didn't want to have coffee."

"I only phoned you then. We didn't see each other. How have you been?" she asked, drawing closer.

He knew very well when he'd last seen her. Thoughts of her had plagued him for days afterward. His pulse was beating faster now at her nearness. *She's so sweet you could spread her on bread,* he thought, using sarcasm to keep his feelings in check. "Great," he answered.

"I saw Ginger and Devin yesterday. They asked about you."

Jack nodded his head slightly and looked away. That must have been a pretty little picnic: Devin, his new wife, and "the other woman."

"I told them that I didn't see you as much as I'd like," she went on, taking a step closer. She was only about three feet away now.

"How's Devin?" he asked, staring at her abruptly. He needed to take the offensive with her before she had any chance to begin to wrap him around her finger again. But when he gazed into the shadowy beauty of her dark, lustrous eyes, it almost took his breath away.

"Fine. He and Ginger are very happy together," she said easily.

He couldn't help but admire her composure. "That must be hard for you to take," he said abrasively.

She lowered her eyes, then raised them to his again. "No, it isn't at all."

"Now that you've lost all your chances with him, you keep trying to start up with me again. Second choice is better than none, is that your philosophy?"

"Jack . . ."

"Well, you can forget it! I don't know why you keep bothering me. I told you, we're through!" He looked away, anger making his breath come faster.

"Jack, I tried to explain once and didn't do a very good job of it. Please try to understand. My interest in him was like a smoke screen for me. I didn't want to deal with the strong feelings I had for you. I knew he loved Ginger. I knew I had no chance with him. But it gave me an escape from the way you were rushing me at the time."

Where's the violin music? Jack thought. She could make a man almost believe her when she wanted to. He was glad Ginger had told him the truth that night weeks ago. Marla had admitted to Ginger that she was interested in Devin. Even if nothing had ever come of it, Marla had been untrue in her heart and mind, and in her intentions. Did she expect him to trust her now? He wasn't stupid.

"So you felt I was rushing you. And you, poor innocent thing, you didn't know what to do! Is that what made you laugh so hard when I mentioned marriage?" Why was he bringing that up? She shouldn't know it was still on his mind, that it still hurt. He'd been managing to play it so cool the last several weeks.

"Some people laugh when they're nervous . . . or afraid," she replied. All at once she reached out and touched his arm. "I'm not laughing anymore." Her warm eyes shone with a rare light as she looked up at him.

Jack backed away, feeling singed. All he could get out was a biting "Is that so!"

"It's true," she said softly. "I would like to marry you."

Silence filled the airy, sunlit room. Jack felt a tremor go through him. *She's tricky, you fool,* he told himself urgently. *Whatever she's up to, don't buy it.*

24

"Sorry. I only make such a rash offer once." He turned from her and walked across the small room.

"And I'm finally giving you my answer," she said, staying where she was, her eyes following him.

He glowered at her. "You gave me your answer over two months ago. You laughed!"

"Yes, but that wasn't an answer. That just meant I wasn't ready to consider the proposal yet. Now I am, and I've thought it over carefully. My answer is yes."

Oh, she's quick! Jack thought. No wonder he'd been taken in by her. She was clever as the devil. But he was on to her ways now. "Well, I've changed my mind!"

He watched Marla slowly look down at the wood floor. She seemed truly sad. He wished he could believe it was real. But she was probably well practiced in using those dramatic eyes of hers.

"Can't we try to be friends, then?" she asked. "You said we could."

"I did?" He couldn't recall ever saying that.

"Yes . . . didn't you?"

"I don't remember it," he said firmly.

"Don't you think we should be?"

See how she's manipulating you? he warned himself. "Not necessarily."

"Well, if we can't be friends, then maybe we ought to get married."

"What the hell kind of logic is that?" he burst out. "Listen, Marla, I don't want to be friends, lovers *or* married. I don't want to have anything to do with you. We're through, finished, kaput! Have I made myself clear?"

She stared at him with clear eyes. "Yes, but I don't believe you. I don't believe you don't want to see me anymore. You remember what we had together as well as I do." Her voice was growing a little uneven.

"What did we have together? A physical attraction, that was all it was. Maybe I got carried away and thought about marriage. But those feelings disappeared when I found out how little I could trust you. Now that all's been said and done, it's clear to me that what we really had together was—nothing!"

Marla stood still for a moment, not saying anything. Her eyes became glassy, and she blinked hard. *Tears?* Jack wondered. *Real tears?* She took a few steps toward him until she was standing in front of him. Now that she was so close, he could see some wetness on her lower lashes, but she was composed as she spoke quietly, her head held high.

"You can tell yourself anything you want, Jack. This is what I'm telling you: I want you back. I *refuse* to let you go. And I promise you that you'll be seeing a lot more of me." She gave him a little smile, then walked around him and went out the door.

Jack was mentally reeling. She wasn't going to let him be? He was in for more of this? *Oh, Lord!*

He walked slowly to a high-backed wood chair in the corner of the room and sat down. This was terrible. The woman who was plaguing him had promised him more of the same!

Why did he feel so exhilarated?

Well, it was *flattering,* he told himself. What healthy man wouldn't feel good when a beautiful woman told him she wasn't going to leave him alone? He was reacting normally, that was all. Just so he didn't let it get the better of him, or else he'd be in the palm of her hand again.

No, he'd keep his common sense, he assured himself. His emotional bruises at her hands still hadn't healed, and he certainly had enough sense to protect himself from getting any more. But how she kept him spinning! He never seemed to know what was going on with her. He had badly misread what he had believed was between them before, and he wasn't sure what was happening now. How could a woman so graceful and lovely be so treacherous?

"Have you seen Jack?" Ginger asked Marla after the waitress had taken their order. They were meeting for lunch at their usual place, the small restaurant on Second Street, across from Marla's real estate office. Ginger owned and ran a kitchen goods shop on First Street. They had been meeting at the café once or twice a week for years and had continued to do so since Ginger's marriage.

"Yes, I saw him a few days ago."

"What happened? What did you say?" Ginger asked.

"Well, I told him I thought we should get married. Of course, he got huffy and said he wasn't interested. Then I simply told him that I refused to let him go," Marla said.

"What did he say to that?"

"Nothing. I walked out then. But I think it took him by surprise. My next strategy is to put him on the defensive."

"You seem pretty sure of yourself," Ginger said, sounding impressed.

"I do? That's good," Marla said with a wan smile. "I don't *feel* too sure of myself, but I guess I put on a good act. It's not easy. I can't take one step out of line, either. I'm going to have to live like a nun to regain his faith in me."

"It wasn't as though you were fast and loose," Ginger said.

"No, but Jack assumes I was—and am," Marla said with a sigh. "I can't really blame him."

"It's not all your fault," Ginger said, dipping her tea bag into the hot water the waitress had just brought. "If Jack had been more sensible and given you a little more breathing space, you probably would have behaved differently."

Marla chuckled a bit at Ginger's logic. "That's a good way to rationalize it!"

"Listen, I went through the same type of thing with Devin. It's not easy to keep your head when you have a man pursuing you, wanting to marry you tomorrow."

"I know, but I don't think men see it that way," Marla said. "And besides . . . I didn't hold back as long as you did with Devin. I just jumped into an affair with Jack, practically without thinking." She shook her head. "It wasn't like me. Not that I was an innocent; after all, I was married briefly when I was eighteen. That was another foolish mistake I ran into headlong. You'd think in over ten years I'd have learned to be a little more cautious."

Marla remembered vividly the heated passions that had risen so quickly between Jack and her at her house the night of their second date. They were sitting on the couch in front of the fire he had helped her build. Jack was toying with her hair as he talked and telling her he'd like to do her portrait sometime. He leaned over then and kissed her lightly on the mouth. She'd never been kissed by a man with a mustache before. She remembered smiling at him, and then leaning toward him to see how it felt again. Suddenly his arms were around her, pulling her against him. He pressed his mouth more ardently against hers and began moving his hands caressingly over her back. She remembered how quickly the heat seemed to flame between them, igniting her desires and his.

It took her by surprise. She hadn't thought she was that attracted to him, though she sensed he was very taken with her. But before she could think it through, his hands were working at the buttons of her blouse, then fondling her breasts so gently it nearly brought tears to her eyes. There was almost a reverence in his touch. No other man had ever handled her in such an exquisite, caring manner. He made her feel so special, as though she were the only woman in the world. He continued, mesmerizing her with his gentleness until, when he wanted everything, she desperately needed fulfillment, too. She realized now that what she had really needed so much was love.

The wistfulness disappeared from Marla's eyes as she remembered where she was—in a restaurant with Ginger. She saw Ginger studying her.

"You're not as unsentimental as you always make yourself out to be, are you?" Ginger said with empathy.

Marla grew a little embarrassed. She wasn't used to allowing her feelings to rise to the surface for all to see and diagnose. In the past her emotions had never been so strong that she couldn't keep them under control. Now she was having increasing difficulty.

"I guess not. Say, do you know anything about cats?" Marla said, eager to change the subject.

"Cats?"

"There's been one coming around my house the last few days. I was wondering if you knew how to get rid of it."

"It doesn't belong to anyone?"

"I don't know. Probably not. It keeps wanting to get into my garbage—usually in the middle of the night."

"Oh, I see." Ginger thought for a moment. "What have you done so far?"

"Well, I've been feeding it leftovers . . ."

"Feeding it!" Ginger started laughing.

"I thought if I gave it food, it would keep out of my garbage." Suddenly Marla realized how ridiculous the excuse sounded. She was fooling herself again.

"Marla, rule number one is if you feed a cat, it's yours!"

"I know. I guess I'm as much of a soft touch for the cat as I was for Jack," Marla admitted.

Ginger chuckled. "Looks like you've got a pet."

"Hardly," Marla said, sighing. "The critter is scared to death of me!"

Marla studiously read what was written on the box, then got out an old bowl and poured some dry cat food into it. It was Monday morning, and she had just been out shopping for groceries. Last night she had had no leftovers to give the cat, except for a saucer of milk, and she was again awakened in the middle of the night by noises around her garbage can.

29

She decided that since she had started feeding the animal, she might as well be efficient about it.

She saw a fleeting glimpse of fluffed white as it ran away when she opened the back door to put out the bowl of dry food. "Here, kitty, kitty." She waited. No response, not even a distant meow. Spending money on a cat she rarely saw and couldn't get near seemed silly. But it wasn't the only foolish thing she'd done in the last few months. She just hoped her plan of action for this afternoon would not fit into the same category.

Several hours later Marla opened the door to Jack's gallery and walked in. The bells on the door rang as she did so. The place seemed empty except for the paintings on the walls and the chair in the corner. She stood there alone for a few minutes.

It was partly cloudy today, but the room, with its high, bare, divided windows, seemed bright. Jack had told her once that he had bought the old house for his gallery because he liked the quality of the light as it streamed through the windows and touched the refinished wood of the floors, window frames and doorjambs. He said it reminded him of the style in which certain Dutch artists had handled light in their seventeenth-century paintings.

Marla, of course, hadn't really known what he was talking about. She had never studied historical works of art, but it was fascinating to listen to him. She hadn't ever met a man who paid so much attention to the atmosphere around him, much less one who could analyze it and even ascribe emotional qualities to it. Jack's way of thinking and his whole frame of reference were very different from her own. It had often made her feel there was a great deal in the world around her she had never learned to appreciate.

All at once she heard footsteps coming down the staircase in the next room. Jack must have been upstairs painting in his studio or doing paperwork in his small office. She took a deep breath to prepare herself. She wasn't used to deliberately picking fights with people, but . . .

"Oh, it's you," Jack said as he suddenly appeared in the doorway to the next room. His voice had a note of impatience in it.

"Yes, it's me. I told you I'd be back to see you." It was good to look at his tall, rangy figure again, even if he wasn't glad to see her. He looked weary, somehow. He had the last time she'd seen him, too. The lines around his eyes looked deeper, and his old air of vitality seemed to have waned. But he looked wonderful to Marla, all the same.

"I was hoping you'd forget that promise," Jack said dourly.

"This isn't a very cordial way to greet a person," Marla said in a nettled tone.

"I told you last week I didn't want to have anything more to do with you. Why are you here?"

"I was thinking we could have dinner together this evening," Marla said smoothly.

"Sorry, I have other plans." Jack's tone had grown frigid.

"Like what, cleaning your brushes?" Marla said, meaning to provoke him.

He stared at her, his eyes hard. "My plans are my business."

"I *see*," she said snappishly. "And I don't even get so much as a thank-you for the invitation!"

"A thank-you? I don't owe you the time of day, Marla!"

She felt herself reel slightly. He could hit hard when he wanted to. "I think the way you've been treating me is abominable! I would think it was beneath your dignity, your —your sense of refinement, to treat a former friend with so much rudeness, no matter what's come between us."

His expression changed, as if she had taken him off-guard. She had gotten his attention, all right. Encouraged, she pressed on with her lecture.

"You keep treating me as though I were dirt you'd swept

out your door. I'm a human being, and I deserve more respect than that. I know after what happened you look upon me as a woman with some sort of tarnished virtue. But what about you? Have you always lived a perfect life? Have you never made a mistake? Who are you to be throwing stones?"

As if at a loss, he stared at her for a moment. Then he said, "I never cheated on you!"

"I never cheated on *you*," she said. "Not really."

"You just thought about it a lot!" he countered in an acrid tone.

"And how do I know what *you* thought about? When we first met, you never stopped talking about all your women friends and all your dinner dates. How do I know I was the only one on your mind all the time?" Let's see him argue that one, she thought.

"Most of my dinner dates were either for business or just to keep in touch with acquaintances," he said. "Once I got involved with you, I didn't have time to see anyone else. And I didn't *want* to see anyone else. Can you say the same?" His eyes and voice challenged her.

She swallowed. He wasn't going to get the better of her. "I've explained all that. We're talking about you now. It strikes me as strange that most of your friends are women. Are you claiming all your dealings with them were pure and totally innocent?"

"I don't have to claim anything to you!"

"Aha! So they weren't."

"I didn't say that!" he shot back.

"You didn't answer the question with a resounding *yes*, either. I bet there were times when your business with these —these acquaintances led to pleasure. Am I right? Be honest," she said, looking him in the eye.

"Maybe. But it's none of your affair."

"When you go around casting aspersions on *my* past and *my* behavior, I think it is!"

Jack leaned tiredly against the doorjamb. "Marla, what's the purpose of all this arguing?"

"Just to point out that you're no paragon of virtue, either. I'm willing to bet there was a time in your life when you had two women on your mind at the same time, whether you were actually involved with them or not. You ought to be able to forgive me for something you've probably done yourself." *There,* she thought with a long exhalation as she finished her speech. She had stated her case.

Jack straightened up and looked down at her, bitterness in his eyes. "I told you I loved you, Marla. I'd never said that to a woman in my life. But I said it to you, and I meant it. And I asked you to be my wife. I'd never asked anyone to marry me before, either. I know you never said you had any similar feelings for me, but I didn't think you'd be chasing someone else when you knew how I felt about you. You claim I'm being rude to you. Well, what you did to me was much worse than rude, Marla. You broke my trust, you broke my illusions about you, you broke my—" He stopped before finishing. His voice had grown rough.

They stood in tense silence for a moment. Marla couldn't look at him. Yes, she had broken his heart. She knew it. There she stood, feeling the heavy weight of guilt all on her shoulders again. She had wronged him, and there was no way she could make him forget it.

"Having an affair with you was a big mistake," he said, his tone resigned. "All I want is my old life back again. It may have been superficial, a lot of social busywork to make myself think I was leading a full life. But there's one thing I'm sure of: It was a hell of a lot better than what I got from you! Now go away and don't bother me anymore."

Marla swallowed back tears. "What about me?" she said, her voice weaker than before. "I need you in my life, not out of it."

"Oh, come now, Marla. You can replace me easily enough. You know how to handle men, how to use your looks and witchery to draw them under your power. You won't have any problem at all," he finished in a cold, tight voice.

"But, Jack . . ." Her voice was nearly a whisper. "I—I—" She wanted to say she loved him. But the word wouldn't come out of her mouth. Somehow she couldn't give voice to such an emotionally charged admission.

"Jack?" A voice from the next room made Marla's eyes widen in shock as she stood there desperately trying to express herself. She had thought they were alone in the building. "Jack? Are you busy, or can you answer a question about the bookkeeping?"

It was a polite, sweet-sounding, feminine voice. Jack immediately turned and went back into the other room. As Marla watched through the doorway, a petite blond woman, probably about Jack's age, came down the steps with some papers in her hands. She smiled as Jack approached.

She was impeccably groomed, her short, pixielike hairstyle perfectly combed, her pastel sweater and skirt tastefully coordinated and rather expensive-looking. The woman appeared to have quite a curvaceous figure, which was very demurely covered. The mauve-and-cream plaid skirt was A-line and hemmed at a proper length, the cashmere sweater elegantly casual and not too form-fitting. She looked much like the sort of upper-middle-class suburban woman who served on the boards of ladies' charitable organizations and attended church teas. Marla had often shown homes to such women from Seattle. They usually came to Whidbey Island to look into a summer home for their families.

The woman's short stature made Jack bend over her shoulder a bit while he studied the paper in her hand. As Marla observed them, her heart began to sink. Jack looked protective as he hovered over the woman, patiently answering her questions. They were both blond, both attractive, both earnest and soft-spoken. They looked like a matched pair.

Repressing a growing feeling of gloom, Marla summoned what remained of her tolerance for pain and walked up to them.

CHAPTER THREE

Before Marla could speak, the woman looked up, smiled apologetically and said, "Oh, I didn't see you. I'm sorry to have interrupted. Was Jack showing you a painting?"

Marla was taken slightly off-guard by her cordial manner. She smiled back. "No, I'm—an old friend of his. I just stopped by. My name is Marla Rosetti." She extended her hand.

The woman took it warmly. "I'm Claire Lyle. My husband was also a friend of Jack's. They went to art school together years ago in New York. Are you an artist, too?"

"No," Marla said. Her eyes brightened a bit. "You and your husband live in the area now?"

Claire dropped her gaze momentarily. "My husband passed away about a year ago." She smiled again. "But Jack's kept in touch with us—my daughter and me—just the same as when Harry was alive."

"I see," Marla replied. "So you stopped by for a visit today?" She hoped the answer would be affirmative but somehow knew it wouldn't be.

Claire glanced at Jack and grinned. "No, I work here," she told Marla. "My daughter's in high school and doesn't really need me much anymore. I mentioned to Jack last week that I'd been thinking of finding some sort of part-time job, and what do you think? He suggested I help him run his gallery!" Claire's blue-green eyes were filled with delight.

"How nice," Marla said, forcing a grin. "I didn't know you needed help, Jack." She turned her tight smile on him.

"I've been wanting more time to paint," he said tersely. "Claire knows a lot about art from her husband. She was a perfect choice. I'm glad she was available." He stared at Marla, his eyes steady and a trifle smug.

Marla looked back at Claire. The woman had an air of lifelong sheltered innocence. Marla guessed she had probably been raised by a well-to-do family in some pleasant neighborhood. After she married, her husband had probably been protective as well. There was a sense of propriety about her, as though naughty thoughts never entered her lovely blond head. "Well," Marla said, trying to sound enthusiastic about Claire's new job, "how many days a week will you work?"

"I thought I'd try three days a week to start with. I have to commute from Seattle, so I'll have to see how it goes. Jack thought that three days would be enough to take care of his bookkeeping and also help with customers on the days I'm here."

"You'll have to be multitalented," Marla said.

"She is," Jack said. "She makes good coffee, too."

"Yes, would you like some?" Claire quickly asked. "We have a pot going upstairs."

"Thank you, I would." Marla noted Jack's look of displeasure at the fact that she would be staying awhile longer. "I thought you told me you didn't drink coffee anymore, Jack," she said sweetly.

He hesitated, obviously reminded of the excuse he had given her.

"Oh, I make brewed decaffeinated, so there's no caffeine," Claire said, her tone of voice motherly. "Jack said he's been having trouble sleeping lately, so of course we can't have him drinking regular coffee anymore."

"Sounds like you take good care of him," Marla said with a smile, though her stomach was turning. The woman was so sugary sweet! It wasn't put on, either, Marla thought. It seemed to be Claire's natural personality—sweet, pretty and pure. *Oh, Lord,* she said to herself. *Will I have to compete with this?*

"Someone should take care of Jack, don't you think? He's been a bachelor for so long," Claire said with a light laugh.

"I suppose you're right," Marla had to agree. Jack looked impatient.

"Come on upstairs and I'll pour you a cup," Claire said. "I've got some homemade cookies, too, though Jack's already eaten half of them."

Marla followed Claire up the stairs, swallowing her pride at having to behave like a mere guest in the gallery. Marla used to have free access to every part of Jack's workplace. Now this stranger was inviting her to have coffee in the studio where Marla and Jack had often spent time together, indeed had even made love one Monday afternoon when their desire for one another could not be denied. After running downstairs to close the shop temporarily, he had led Marla to the couch he sometimes used when painting portraits. There he had tenderly undressed her and made love to her. It was an afternoon she would never forget.

But, of course, Claire wouldn't know about that. Claire would probably have difficulty believing that intelligent, educated people would engage in such unbridled behavior, especially in the middle of the day.

Don't be so catty, Marla told herself. Claire was a very nice woman. Marla just wished she hadn't had such a yen to go back to work.

"Do you live on the island?" Claire asked Marla as they walked into the large upstairs studio. Jack silently followed them in.

"Yes," Marla replied. "Not too far from here."

Claire chuckled. "I can imagine. Langley's such a small town. What line of work is your husband in?"

Marla almost spilled the hot coffee Claire had just given

38

her. "I'm not married," she said, feeling slightly embarrassed, though she didn't know why she should. "I'm a real estate agent. My office is over on Second Street."

"Oh," Claire said. Her benign smile stayed on her lips, which had a perfectly applied coating of pink lipstick, but her high, bell-like voice had a new tone in it. "A career woman. How interesting," she said. She glanced for the first time at Marla's ringless left hand. After a moment she asked, "Real estate agents have to work all sorts of odd hours, don't they? Do you like that?"

"Marla loves it," Jack muttered. He turned away from them and walked to his worktable.

Jack had never liked the late hours Marla had to keep. It had been a bone of contention between them when they were involved in their affair. "I—can't say I like it," Marla answered Claire, "but it's what I have to do for my job." She glanced at Jack, but he was checking some brushes on the table. In truth, she was growing tired of her job and its hours. She longed to tell that to Jack, to let him know that she would be willing to make some adjustments. In the past, stubbornly clinging to her independence, she had told him she would change nothing for him or for the sake of their relationship. She wished she could explain to him that her attitude was softening, but she knew Jack wouldn't listen.

All three were silent for a few moments. Claire seemed thoughtful now. Marla guessed what she was thinking—that Marla was single, not half of a married pair that Jack was friends with, as Claire had apparently assumed. Marla wondered whether, if Claire had noticed her ringless left hand sooner, she would have been so eager to invite her up for coffee.

"Your cookies look good," Marla said to break the silence.

"Please have one," Claire said. She lifted the plate toward Marla. Marla could easily picture her as the perfect wife, keeping a nice home, raising her daughter well, cooking nourishing meals for her husband, being active in the community. She was what Marla could never be, what she would not be if she could. Marla cherished her freedom and, living free, sometimes made mistakes. This woman was dutiful and apparently had made few mistakes in her life. In a word, Claire was reliable, a description Jack would never apply to Marla.

"Mmm, they are good," Marla said after taking a bite of one. "You'll have to give me the recipe." Why did she say that? Marla asked herself. She hadn't baked cookies since she was twelve. Was she trying to impress Jack with the idea that she too could be a good homemaker? Jack would see through that in a minute. But then again . . . maybe he wouldn't.

"I haven't made cookies lately. My specialty is soufflés," she told Claire, feigning an air of pride. She had, in fact, made a soufflé once, years ago. It was in a cooking class she had taken and soon dropped out of, due to boredom.

"Really?" Claire said, sounding impressed. "I've always heard soufflés were tricky to make."

"Not much harder than an omelet, once you get the hang of it," Marla said, as if she spoke from experience. Actually she *was* handy at making omelets. Hamburgers, omelets and frozen dinners were the quickest and easiest things she had found to cook for herself when she got home in the evening after a long day at work. On her days off she occasionally went so far as to make a casserole, but that was the extent of Marla's cooking expertise—or interest.

"What kinds of soufflés do you make?" Claire asked.

"Yes, what kind do you make, Marla?" Jack echoed waspishly.

"Chicken," Marla said without batting an eyelash.

"Really." Claire sounded genuinely interested. "Do you share your recipes? I'd love to have that one."

"I hope it's better than the chicken casserole you make," Jack said.

"Oh, worlds better," Marla replied, directing her gaze toward him. "That's why I've never bothered cooking a soufflé for you. You wouldn't have known the difference."

Claire glanced at them both and seemed self-conscious. She was undoubtedly beginning to wonder if there was something between Jack and Marla.

Marla turned to Claire again. "You'll find that Jack will eat anything. His taste buds are very nondiscriminating. A chicken soufflé or a chicken casserole, it's all the same to him."

"Which explains why I ate any of your cooking at all," Jack said.

Marla ignored the remark. "Of course I'll give you my recipe—if you'll give me yours for these cookies," she said to Claire with a smile.

"I'd be happy to," Claire replied. She seemed a little suspicious of the mixed vibrations in the atmosphere, but she maintained her cordial manner.

"Well, I'd better be going," Marla said. She shook hands with Claire. "Good-bye, Jack. I'll be seeing you." Jack barely nodded and looked away dourly. Obviously he was having difficulty keeping up appearances for Claire's sake. Marla quickly walked out.

"A goody-goody," Marla said, describing Claire to Ginger and Devin that evening at their home. After dinner she had called and asked if she could drop in. She was looking for some moral support.

"She doesn't sound very interesting," Devin said optimistically as they sat around the fireplace. "Men are usually more attracted to women with some spark and unpredictability. If she's as you describe, I doubt a man like Jack would prefer her."

"He might, since he feels I wasn't true to him. He wouldn't have any doubts about Claire being faithful," Marla said. She shifted her position slightly in the large armchair and sighed.

"But a woman like that would insist on marriage," Ginger, who sat on the couch beside Devin, said. "You think he would go so far as to marry her?"

Marla shrugged. "I don't know. I'm afraid, if Claire had anything to say about it, he would."

"So you think she's angling for a second husband," Devin surmised.

"Well, she bakes chocolate chip cookies and brews decaffeinated coffee especially for him. She already acts like she's half-owner of the gallery," Marla said, her jealousy showing a bit. "And the worst part is, she's going to be seeing him at least three days a week. *I'm* lucky to connive a way to see him once a week. And even then he spits fire at me."

"What happened to your plan to put him on the defensive?" Ginger asked.

"Oh, it worked," Marla replied. "I had him on the defensive for about five seconds. Then he gave me both barrels. He said he wants his old bachelor's life back again and ordered me not to bother him anymore."

"Well," Devin said, "at least if he wants to be free, he won't take up seriously with this Claire."

"I suppose that might be true," Marla said, her tone brightening. "Unless, of course, he does it to protect himself from me." Her voice became downcast again.

"You've got to get back into his life, before she can gain a strong foothold on him," Devin said.

"That's what I keep thinking, but I'll be darned if I can figure out how," Marla said. She rubbed the side of her slender nose with her forefinger.

All three were thoughtful for several moments. A log sputtered in the fireplace. Ginger murmured, "He once wanted to paint your portrait. Too bad you can't take him up on that now."

"Yes," Marla said, resting her chin on her hand as she leaned to one side in the armchair. "Then he'd have to see me for several sittings, at least." She took her hand from her chin and sat up straighter. "In fact, that's a wonderful idea."

Ginger smiled, but looked unsure. "How could you ever convince him to do your portrait, though?"

Marla twisted her mouth to one side briefly, making an amusing face. "Beats me. But if there's a way, I'll find it." After a further moment of thought, she said, "Ginger, do you have a French cookbook?"

When Marla got home later, she turned on the back porch light and opened the door. The dish of cat food on her doorstep was empty. As she reached to take it in, she saw, peeking around the corner of her house, a little white head with round eyes and big ears.

"Well, hello," she said, talking to the cat. "Kitty, kitty, kitty?"

The cat did not budge. Quickly she went in, got some more cat food to refill the dish, then went to the door again and stooped down on the small porch. "Still hungry? Here's more food," she said as she ran her fingers through the dry food pellets in the bowl. She held her breath as the cat began to move forward. It stopped then and retreated back to the corner. Marla called softly to it once more. The animal moved forward again, then retreated.

This continued for about ten minutes. Marla was ready to give up when the cat finally moved closer than it had ever come before—about three feet away. She slowly edged the bowl toward the cat, then moved back inside the open door. As she kept perfectly still, the cat cautiously moved toward the bowl and began eating. It looked up at her every few seconds to be sure she was making no move. When it had finished eating, it sat and stared at her for a short while, its eyes like two circles. Then it walked off into the darkness.

Marla smiled to herself as she closed the door. At last she had made some progress getting the cat—or kitten, for it seemed about half-grown—to trust her. If she used the same technique with Jack, would it have the same result?

Marla allowed a few days to go by, then at the end of the week she went back to Jack's gallery on her lunch hour. The evening before she had made some preliminary preparations: She had copied down a recipe from Ginger's cookbook, and she had called her mother, Gina Rosetti, in Seattle.

The bells on the front door jingled as she entered. In moments she heard footsteps coming down the stairs. Marla braced herself. This wouldn't be easy.

"You again," Jack muttered when he saw her. He immediately slowed his stride across the room.

"Claire wanted that recipe for chicken soufflé, so I brought it for her," Marla said innocently. "Is she here today?"

"Upstairs," he said. "I can give it to her." He held out his hand.

Marla opened up her handbag, took out a three-by-five card and gave it to him.

"I'll see that she gets it," he said. He turned back toward the staircase. "Good-bye."

"Wait. I—had something to ask you," Marla said quickly. She had the urge to move toward him and close the space he had put between them. Remembering her technique with the cat, she held herself back.

"What?" he said impatiently.

She took a quick, deep breath. "I'd like you to do a portrait of me," she said, sounding bright and sure of herself. But within her slender rib cage, her heart was pounding.

His brows drew together. "You'd like *what?*" he said warily.

"A painting of me. It's for my mother, actually. She told me she would love to have one for a Christmas present." Marla had called her mother to ask her if she'd like such a gift, and her mother had enthusiastically agreed, so Marla wasn't lying.

"Forget it," he said.

44

"I can't forget it. She has her heart set on it," Marla insisted.

"Find another artist, then." Jack began to go up the stairs when he found Claire coming down them.

"Claire!" Marla said with a broad smile. She walked toward the staircase. "How nice to see you! I brought the recipe. Jack has it."

"How kind of you to remember," Claire said in her soft, warm voice.

"I doubt if kindness had much to do with it," Jack muttered as he handed the card to Claire.

Claire, genuinely pleased, didn't seem to hear him. "I'll have to try it this weekend," she said as she paused to glance over the recipe. She was wearing a lavender blouse with a navy-and-lavender print skirt. Her blond hair was perfectly combed. Marla suddenly felt windblown from the walk over and tucked in her blouse under her tan suit jacket, then pushed back her long hair. Darn! She should have looked in her purse mirror before walking in.

"Should I use an eggbeater or a wire whisk to beat the eggs?" Claire asked.

"Oh—either," Marla replied. She wasn't entirely sure what a wire whisk was.

"Actually, I probably could use my food processor, couldn't I?" Claire said, looking up at Marla now. Her eyes were bright with interest.

"I don't see why not." All Marla knew about food processors was that they were expensive, and that she didn't want one. After all, if she invested that much money in one, she'd just be obligated to use it. As for beating eggs, all Marla ever used was a fork. "How's your new job going?" she asked Claire, hoping to avoid any further questions about the recipe.

"Just fine. Jack teaches me something new every day. There's a lot more to learn about running a gallery than I ever dreamed."

"I was just asking him to do a portrait of me," Marla said, smiling at Claire. She didn't dare glance at Jack.

"You were?" Claire seemed a trifle hesitant. Marla guessed Claire wasn't sure yet whether she should look upon Marla as a potential rival.

"Yes, for my mother. She'd like it for Christmas. She's a widow and I'm her only daughter, so . . . well, you're a mother; you can probably understand her feelings even better than I."

Claire's eyes softened. "Of course I can. It's sweet that you would take the time to have one made. Jack always asks for four or five long sittings. When will you start on it?"

Jack, listening to the conversation, moved to the other side of the room and, with a glowering expression, looked out the window.

"That's just it," Marla said. "Jack refused to do it."

Claire looked shocked. "He did?" She turned her eyes to the man by the window. "Why, Jack?"

"I'm all booked up," he said, looking at neither of them.

"But I was just glancing at your schedule awhile ago. You have some free time in the next couple of weeks," Claire said.

Jack said nothing for a moment. Marla could sense his resentment rising. "I must have been thinking of last week." He hesitated for a few seconds, as the two women watched him expectantly. "All right. You can go ahead and book her," he said to Claire. "Three sittings will be enough." He went to the front door then and walked out of the gallery.

Claire seemed taken aback by his abrupt departure, but she invited Marla upstairs to make the appointments. As they agreed on dates and times, Marla's feeling of triumph was mixed with apprehension. Jack had acquiesced much more easily than she had expected. She had known he would be hesitant, in Claire's presence, to refuse to do a portrait for no apparent reason. Marla had counted on that. But was

46

Claire's high regard so important to him that he would give in like a lamb?

Outside, Jack was walking briskly down the sidewalk toward the wood stairs that led to the beach. *God, Marla is unscrupulous!* he thought. Getting Claire on her side! She knew how to play every card in her hand. Claire was so naive, she'd never suspect anyone could have ulterior motives. A Christmas present for her widowed mother!

Why had he agreed to it? Because he couldn't think of any graceful way out of the situation, he told himself. He should have told Claire he had planned to use the spare time painting seascapes, he thought now. It would have made sense. The whole reason he had hired Claire was so he could have more time to himself to paint. Of course, it might not have seemed sensible to turn down a commissioned portrait. Well, what difference would it have made what Claire thought? He didn't owe her any explanations. *He* was the artist; *he* owned the gallery. He should have simply said he didn't want to do Marla's portrait, period.

He was at the bottom of the old wooden steps now, looking out at the wide beach and forested Camano Island across the cold waters of Saratoga Passage. The tide was out, giving a barren look to the rocky beach. The sky was overcast—like his life since he had broken up with Marla. He knew why he hadn't refused to do her portrait, why he gave in without a fight. He *wanted* to paint her, always had, since the first day he saw her.

Lately he'd thought that if he painted her, it might get her out of his system. Maybe it would. At the sittings he would be indifferent toward her. He'd channel all his feelings for her into the painting, and then he'd be done with her. She might not like the portrait—he knew it would show her as he saw her, reflecting all the hurt, shattered hopes and bitterness he felt. Well, so what? He could never guarantee that his clients would like his work. If she hated the portrait, so much the better. Maybe then she'd leave him alone for good.

CHAPTER FOUR

Jack was arranging his tubes of oil paints and his brushes, attending to details, trying to make this sitting as much like any other as he could. That raven-haired siren wasn't going to get the better of him. He wished Claire were here today, but it was one of her days off. Marla would have had to behave herself if Claire were around. But, then, Marla was skillful at using people, especially one as trusting as Claire. Claire's presence might only have complicated things. This way he was free to tell Marla off if he needed to, and he wouldn't have to worry about shocking his kind-hearted employee.

He didn't intend to show his anger, however. It might lead Marla to think he still loved her—and he knew he didn't. He was going to stick to his plan to be indifferent to her, channeling all emotion into his painting. Then he would sell her the portrait and say good-bye to his resentment and painful memories. They could all go hang together at her mother's house.

The bells on the front door downstairs jingled. He went out to the head of the stairs. "Come on up to the studio," he called. He walked back into the large room without pausing for Marla's response. While he waited, he tensed as he glanced about the room. Unframed paintings were set along one wall, either drying or waiting to be framed and put on display downstairs. There was a straight-back wood chair, a plush velvet stuffed chair and a sofa, all of which he used for various portraits, unless he decided to have the client pose standing. A flush came over him when he glanced at the long beige sofa. He had once used it to make love to Marla, one afternoon when he couldn't keep himself from her. Well, he'd just have to put that out of his . . . No. No, let her pose on it. Let her know that their past didn't matter anymore. Let her understand, and understand thoroughly, that he had put it all behind him.

When Marla walked into the room, he was shifting the couch into place toward the center of the room, where the light from the high windows was best. She was wearing a long black taffeta skirt and a white blouse with long sleeves and an open collar. The neckline was demure, though it made a V to the hollow between her breasts, where a pearl button held the silky, opaque material in place. If she had been a buxom woman, the blouse would have shown cleavage. But Marla had small breasts . . . small and exquisite . . .

Jack gave himself a mental shake. "Nice outfit," he said coldly. "I'm surprised at your choice."

She smiled. He thought she seemed hesitant, but he didn't look at her long enough to be sure. His paints needed arranging.

"I had trouble deciding what to wear," she said. Her voice was always so soft and refined. How could she be the sort of woman she was and still have a voice like that? he asked himself in annoyance. "I had these in my closet, and it seemed like the type of thing I've seen women wear in portraits."

"It's fine," he muttered, squeezing paints onto his oblong wood palette.

"Is it?" she said, sounding unsure. "You said you were surprised."

"Surprised that *you* could come up with something so classy," he said sarcastically.

"Oh." Her tone was quiet.

Damn. He hadn't been going to let his resentment show. Indifferent; he was supposed to be indifferent. She was just another client. "I should have discussed with you what to wear. I usually do," he said, using a calm, detached manner now. "But what you've chosen will do very well." He glanced up at her. "In fact, it enhances your coloring and features nicely," he said, now sounding very much the professional that he was. He quickly looked back at his paints and brushes, though, carrying her image with him. She was so beautiful. White always looked wonderful on her, offsetting her soft olive complexion and highlighting her large eyes. Her dark brown hair tumbled gracefully over her small shoulders, shining, thick and luxurious. She was an artist's dream. And finally he was going to paint her.

Oh, God, he thought. He had been afraid he would be too full of hurt and animosity to do an acceptable portrait of her, and now he was going in the opposite direction, becoming overeager and excited at the prospect. He had to get control of himself. She was just a woman. Just another woman.

No, she wasn't. Not to him. He had to be truthful with himself or he'd never get back on an even keel. *All right,* he told himself sternly, setting a large clean canvas on the easel. *When you get carried away looking at her, remember how untrue she was. When you get angry, remember her beauty. And think of her beauty only in an artistic sense, you fool!*

"How shall I pose?" Marla said.

"What? Oh . . ." He'd forgotten he'd left her standing there. Marla wasn't the type of woman who usually waited for direction. She seemed a little subdued today. "On the couch," he said tersely, motioning toward it.

He noticed she paused for a moment before walking toward it. She sat down carefully at one end of it. "Like this?"

He raised his eyes from his palette where he had squeezed out an assortment of appropriate colors. He'd really have to look at her now, to study her pose; it couldn't be avoided.

She was lovely sitting there just as she was, one hand on the arm of the couch. Her slender body always seemed to move into unconsciously graceful poses. He had often noticed that about her, and it had fascinated him. But the pose wasn't the best it could be. It didn't show her quiet determination and strength, the traits he had learned to both respect and resent. Yes, he had to get that in, he thought bitterly.

"How about standing up again, then propping yourself on the arm of the couch. Yes, like that. Now, one hand in your lap, the other across the back of the couch. Fine. Just like that."

"I'm not sure how long I can sit this way. My leg may fall asleep after a while," she said.

"I'll give you a break every now and then," Jack said. He set about sketching her on the canvas first, the flow of her long skirt, the small waist, the tilt of her shoulders, the supple arms, the regal lift of her head. Everything about her was perfectly proportioned, like a Dresden doll. She was as fragile and feminine as a man could want, but willful instead of winsome, sensual instead of sweet. He had certainly learned that. Except today she was—well, she seemed winsome and sweet. It must be an act, part of her scheme to get him back under her spell. He wasn't going to let himself buy it.

"Can we talk?" she asked after he had been sketching in silence for several minutes.

"If you must."

"Would it bother you?"

"I've painted chatterbox women before. Just don't move." Why did he say that? he asked himself in annoyance. He should have told her no. But he wanted to know what she was thinking, why she was being different today. He needed to know what she was up to, he rationalized.

"How's business been?" she asked.

"Fine."

"Is Claire working out well as your assistant?"

"Yes."

51

Her tone grew lighter. "Have you gained weight from eating her chocolate chip cookies?"

"No . . . I don't know." He was perturbed at the question.

"Well, at least that was more than a one-word answer," she said, amused. There was a honeyed quality in her voice that he'd not often heard her use before. He liked it—and he knew that was dangerous.

She was quiet for a while. Jack sketched on. The rough outline of her figure and the end of the couch were done. He was working more carefully with a pencil on the details of her face, the large, expressive eyes, the soft lips . . .

"I have a cat now," she said all at once, disturbing his thought pattern. "I guess it's mine. I've been feeding it and it's getting more friendly . . ."

A cat. That was fitting, Jack thought as he listened and worked. Some women were like cats. They won't come when you call, then come when you don't call—just like Marla had come back to him.

"So it's been sleeping on my back porch lately," she was saying, "but I still haven't been able to get too close to it."

Smart cat, Jack thought dourly.

"Have you ever had a cat?" she asked.

"No."

"A dog?"

"When I was a kid."

"What kind?"

"A mutt."

"Was it a big dog?" she asked.

"No."

"Small?"

"Medium," he said, growing impatient. "Black and white. Long ears, short tail."

"Sounds cute."

Jack didn't reply. She was sure on a conversational streak, he thought. It used to be the reverse. He did most of the talking and she listened, saying little. If she thought she could get him to open up like that again, she was badly mistaken.

He picked up his palette and began to put color on the canvas, starting with the rich dark browns of her hair.

Marla watched him, wondering what the portrait was like so far. She was anxious to know how he would paint her, how he saw her, though she was half afraid he might paint her as a Salem witch being burned at the stake.

He was so difficult to talk to. Before she arrived, she had decided that the best thing to do was to try to build a friendship with him, if she could. They had never really been friends, having skipped that step by going immediately into an affair. Trust was something they had never learned.

This was her chance to start again from the beginning, she felt. If she could do it right this time, she would first try to gain his friendship, then his trust. Later their physical relationship would fall back into place naturally enough—except that, of course, she now intended to marry him.

So she had carefully chosen her long skirt and demure white blouse, trying to be the image of respectability, and she was doing her best to be as pleasant and affable as she could. But so far Jack was like a pillar of granite, hard and impenetrable. She had only three sittings to make a crack in that pillar, and the first one was already fleeing by.

"Can I take a short break? My back's getting a little stiff," she said.

"Yes." He continued working on the painting and didn't look up.

Marla stood and stretched, then slowly walked toward him. She came around the easel to stand next to him, but before she could look at the painting, he turned abruptly.

"Stay back. I don't want you to see it before it's finished," he said, perturbed.

"Okay." She retreated a few steps. "Why not?"

"I always do it that way," he said. "Some clients get picky

53

about this and that, not realizing that the portrait's going to be altogether different by the time it's done."

"Shouldn't I check to see if I like the pose, though, before you get too far along? I thought the client usually had some say about that," she said.

Jack did not respond for several moments and continued to work. She knew she had made a valid point; after all, she was paying him for a custom-made product, so to speak. Finally he mumbled in a growling tone, "You'll like the pose."

Marla decided to let that be the end of that discussion. It made her wonder even more exactly how he was portraying her. For her mother's sake, she hoped he would at least make her look pretty, however else he crucified her on canvas.

"Don't *you* take a break?" she asked.

"No."

"Can I make you some coffee? I see Claire left the can of decaf out and the filters," she said.

"You wouldn't know how," he said sarcastically. "You can't even make decent instant coffee. I never could figure out if it was because you don't know how to measure a teaspoon into the cup or if you don't know how to boil water."

Marla ignored the remarks. It was true, though, that when he used to come over to her place, he had often said that the coffee was a little weak or it wasn't hot enough. He always drank it, however. "We have an electric coffee maker like this at work. I can run it," she said confidently.

"If it'll keep you busy for a few minutes, go ahead," he said with a sigh.

She walked to the small table near the door, where the coffee maker was. Actually what she had told Jack hadn't been entirely accurate. The automatic coffee brewer at her office was much bigger than the one now in front of her. And even at that, she had never made the coffee at work herself.

54

The office secretary always did it. But how difficult could it be?

She took a new filter paper out of the box and figured out how to fasten it into the funnel that held the coffee grounds. After reading the directions on the coffee can, she found the measuring spoon and measured the correct amount for four cups. She took the glass decanter to the small bathroom off the office and filled it to the correct measuring line from the sink, then brought it back to the coffee maker. She poured it into the top of the machine, as she had often seen the secretary do, then placed the decanter on the warming pad below the funnel.

There, she thought, feeling a little proud of herself that she had accomplished it all without having to ask any questions. "It should be ready in a few minutes," she told Jack. "How's the portrait coming?" She began to walk toward him.

"Fine. When the coffee's done, you can go back to posing," he said, sounding impatient.

"All right." She looked back at the coffee maker. Her heart sank as she saw very pale amber water flowing slowly into the decanter from the funnel. "Oh, no," she said softly.

"What's the matter?"

"Nothing," she said, going to the machine. What had gone wrong? She thought she must have done everything that needed to be done.

"What the hell did you do?"

She turned and saw Jack looking around his easel at the anemic coffee she had produced. "I don't know. Maybe the machine is broken," she said.

With a heavy sigh Jack set down his brush and palette on the worktable next to him and walked over to the coffee maker. After looking at it for a second, he said, "You have to turn it on, silly!" He flipped the switch from Off to Brew. Immediately a small light went on and the machine began making noises. He poured the water in the decanter back into the top.

"Oh," Marla said, feeling pretty stupid. She had assumed it was always on, like the one at work seemed to be. "Sorry."

Jack looked at her and said nothing for a moment. He was trying to contain his impatience and anger, she supposed. When he said, "Go back and take your pose," it was in a much milder tone than she had expected.

Quickly she went back to the couch and sat on the arm as she had been. She watched him go back to his easel. Before he picked up his brush, he ran his fingers over his forehead, not in the way he would if he had a headache, but as if he was shaken or unsettled about something. When he looked up at her, though, his eyes had the same distance and coldness they had had before.

"Lean more to the left," he told her. She complied, and he began to put his brush to the canvas again.

She said nothing for a while, watching him work. The easel was angled to one side, and she had a three-quarter view of him. He was wearing a plain blue shirt, the sleeves rolled to the elbow, and blue jeans. He usually wore old clothes when he painted; he wasn't the most careful person when he was absorbed in his work, and his shirts often acquired a few paint stains. Though he was handsome when he was dressed in a suit or blazer, Marla liked him best like this. His mustache, as usual, was a bit overgrown, and his hair was mussed from unconsciously raking his fingers through it as he worked.

This was the real Jack Whiting, she thought, the true essence of the man, not the polished, talkative socializer she had at first thought him to be. *That* man she had found to be a little tiresome, though amusing, in a way. She hadn't seen the complex and profound depths of the very masculine personality that lay just beneath his easygoing surface—not until the night they had unexpectedly made love. Suddenly she had found herself involved with a much more sensitive, exciting and demanding man than she had ever dreamed existed.

How she wanted that man back again now, not this grumbling, resentful and wary artist who looked up at her every now and then with cold, calculating eyes. He couldn't have lost all feeling for her. Not now, when she felt more love and need for him than she had ever known she could feel for anyone. Somewhere deep inside he must still love her a little, even if she had treated him badly.

Marla blinked back the tears that misted her eyes. Jack hadn't noticed, she was sure. She tried to think of something to say to begin a conversation. They'd never become friends if they didn't talk. She started telling him about her job, then, and the houses she was currently marketing. Jack seemed to listen with half an ear.

"I'm beginning to get a little tired of the long hours," she said. It was an opportunity to tell him she was willing to be more flexible and less dogged about her work. "I'm hoping to be able to cut back and have more time to myself, or even get out of the real estate business altogether."

"Really," Jack said. Her spirits sank. He sounded suspicious, as though he thought she was telling him that in order to get him back, not because she honestly felt that way about her job. But she did.

"Yes, really," she said.

"What would you do?"

"I don't know yet. Ginger . . ." She hesitated about bringing this up. It seemed too tender a subject to mention to him at the moment, but she continued anyway. "Ginger said at lunch last week that she and Devin want to have a baby. She knows I've been thinking of quitting real estate, and she asked if I would consider buying her shop. Of course she won't sell it until—and if—she actually becomes pregnant. But it's given me something to think about."

"What—getting pregnant or buying her shop?" Jack said.

She thought the remark was cruel. "Buying the shop,"

Marla replied, hiding her hurt feelings. She might understand why Jack had come to the conclusion that she was easy with men, but he didn't have to make such below-the-belt comments. It was probably because she had mentioned Devin. Wouldn't Jack ever forget her foolish behavior?

"You don't think it would be a little ludicrous for you to run a shop that sells kitchen goods?" Jack said.

Marla had no answer for a moment. So far she had only considered the business aspects of buying Ginger's shop—whether she could get a bank loan, if she would make as much as she did from real estate, and that the hours would be better. She began to laugh. "No, I hadn't thought of it," she admitted. "But I won't have to know how to cook. I'd just be selling things like pots and pans, place mats and novelty salt and pepper shakers."

"What if someone came in and asked you what size pan they'd need to make a quiche or some fancy dessert? You might be able to fool someone as trusting as Claire into thinking that you know what you're talking about. But it would catch up with you sooner or later," he said. Though she didn't like his words, she noted that at least his tone was more kind now, almost like a brother giving advice to his sister.

Marla took a long, thoughtful breath. She had no good reply. So he'd seen through her all along when she'd told Claire she made soufflés. His comment about Claire's ingenuousness didn't make her feel any better, either.

"Ginger could teach me . . ."

"Marla, let's face it," he said, sounding impatient again. "You're no good in the kitchen. You could never learn all you'd need to know, because cooking isn't something that interests you. Even if you tried, you'd soon hate it. Yes, you're capable of running a business, but not *that* business."

Marla bowed her head, realizing that everything he said was true. She would never be the homemaker type, the hug-the-hearth sort of wife Claire would make.

"Tilt your chin up. I can't paint you when you're sagging like that," Jack said, his tone sharp.

She lifted her head again and straightened her back. Her eyes had a moist sheen to them.

Jack tried not to notice her glassy eyes, but he couldn't help it. His brush seemed to move automatically to the dark eyes in the portrait. He made several deft strokes. Suddenly he wanted to capture that expression. He had always thought she was beautiful, but never so much as now, with all that brave sorrow in her gaze.

It was getting to him. He wanted to be indifferent toward her, but how could he? She was trying so hard to be what she thought he wanted her to be. In spite of the cold heart he meant to have toward her, she touched him and moved him. He almost wanted to console her.

Almost. No, he wasn't that stupid. Maybe she was sorry she had chased after Devin, maybe she meant to turn over a new leaf, maybe she did care for Jack to whatever depth a woman like Marla could care for a man; it didn't mean he should risk getting involved with her again.

He had barely recovered from his first encounter with her, and a woman like her could always become wayward again. Marla, Jack had concluded, behaved like some men, to whom the chase was everything: Once the object of desire had been captured, interest was quickly lost and a search began for someone new. It was what she had, in fact, done—tried to turn to Devin when she was growing bored in her affair with Jack. And now that Jack had deserted her, her interest in him was rekindled.

Perhaps she was amoral. Perhaps she didn't understand her own motivations, Jack thought later, after Marla had left and he was alone in his studio with her unfinished portrait. She wasn't really so treacherous as he had been telling himself. After seeing her today, he felt a little ashamed of the things he had thought and said about her. His crack about getting pregnant was certainly uncalled for, and he wished now he hadn't said it. It was just that she had mentioned Devin. He ought to let go of his jealousy. He could believe now that Marla had never really cared for Devin. Devin had only been a passing fancy. That was the trouble with Marla: All men were passing fancies.

Jack picked up a rag to clean his brushes. No, Marla wasn't a tricky femme fatale. She was just beautiful and confused. He felt sorry for her now. Perhaps he could try to talk to her, get her to understand herself better and see why she behaved as she did with men. He guessed he still cared for her enough to try to counsel her. If someone didn't help her, she would certainly be headed for an unhappy life, Jack thought, shaking his head. Such a lovely, intelligent woman. It was a shame.

╳ It began to rain shortly after Marla returned home late that afternoon. She looked out onto her back porch and saw that the cat's bowl was empty again. As she opened the door to take the bowl in, the cat suddenly appeared from beneath some bushes near the house. Its fur got wet as it ran toward the porch. Marla hurried in to refill the bowl. Instead of setting it outside again, she put it down on the kitchen floor a few feet from the open door. The little cat watched her, then looked up with questioning eyes.

"Come on, kitty. Don't you want to come in out of the rain? Your food will just get wet if I put it outside again."

After several minutes of coaxing the cat finally began to move toward the door, meowing as it did so. It was a jittery creature, moving from side to side as much as it moved forward. As it crossed the threshold into the kitchen, it stopped for a moment. Marla put out her hand to try to pet it. The cat jumped back and spit. She withdrew her hand and shook the bowl of food lightly. After a few moments the cat cautiously moved toward her, alternately meowing and spitting, as if wanting to come closer but afraid at the same time. At last, when the cat was far enough in, she shut the door.

She simply watched the animal eat from the bowl. It was a pretty little cat, entirely white, with big gold eyes, long fur and a feathery tail. Its paws were large, giving it a slightly clumsy appearance like a clown, and its eyes had a mischievous look. When she reached out again to stroke it gently as it crunched on the dry food, it suddenly responded with a loud purr that made Marla smile. At last she and the cat had made friends.

The rain continued, and she kept the cat in all night. It was the first time she had ever had an animal in the house. After wandering about, exploring her home all evening, it followed her into the bedroom when she went to bed. She was surprised to see it curl up beside her when she got under the covers. It was nice to have some company while she slept.

When she awoke early in the morning, however—to the sound of pattering paws and something being knocked over —she discovered all the havoc one small cat could create. Two potted plants on her kitchen windowsill were knocked down, one broken. In the living room, the drapes showed signs of having been climbed and a lace doily from a side table had been pulled down and mangled. The knickknacks on top had been knocked onto the carpet. In the bathroom the roll of toilet tissue had been unraveled and thoroughly shredded by ten sharp claws.

But when the cat came over and brushed up against her legs, purring, Marla was hard put to remain angry. She bent to pet it, and a few minutes later she was deciding on a name.

"I call him Max," she was telling Claire two days later. They were up in Jack's studio. While Jack was preparing his paints, Claire had started a conversation with Marla, as if she felt it her duty to entertain Jack's clients and make them comfortable. Marla had hoped it would be another of Claire's days off, but when she arrived that morning and saw her, she quickly decided to make the best of it. "I thought it would be a good name for him when he's a big, grown-up cat."

"But what if it turns out to be a female?" Claire asked with a smile. "It's hard to tell what gender cats are. At least, I can never tell."

I can believe that, Marla thought. "I got a good look at him the other day, and I'm sure he's male," Marla said. She glanced at Jack and caught his disapproving eye. As she looked back at Claire, she blushed slightly. "Did you try the chicken soufflé recipe?" she asked, deciding to switch to a safer subject.

"Yes, thank you again. It was delicious."

"I'm ready to start," Jack said. His voice was a little impatient, as if he were tired of the female chatter. "Take your pose, Marla. Claire, will you be doing the bookkeeping in the office?" It was more of a directive than a question.

"Yes, and I'll see to any customers who might come in," Claire said, walking toward the door. "There's coffee and cookies, Marla, if you want some." When she reached the door she looked back at Jack. "Shall I leave this door open?"

"No. Close it."

"All right," she said and pulled it shut behind her. Marla thought she detected a hint of disappointment in Claire's dulcet voice.

Marla, propped on the arm of the couch again, smiled at Jack. "You like to work in peace?"

"Yes," he replied. He studied the portrait for a moment. "Your hand was closer to your knee last time. Yes, that's better, but shake out the ruffle on your sleeve so it covers your hand more. Okay."

Marla allowed him to work in silence for a while and used the time to try to think of a good way to get him into conversation again. She felt she had made some progress with him last time, but much too little to suit her. There were only two more sittings, including this one, and she felt the press of time.

He surprised her then by starting a conversation himself. "How do you feel today?" he asked.

"Great," she said, smiling. "And you?"

"I thought you seemed a little downcast last time," he went on, ignoring her question.

"I did?" She thought a second. "Oh, well, you had burst my bubble about taking over Ginger's shop, that's all," she said lightly. She didn't want to let on how inadequate he had made her feel.

"It's good to have a dream in life," he said. "It was a fine idea; I just think you need to find the right kind of business to run, one that's suited to your interests."

His voice was gentle and understanding. Did he regret what he had said about her aptitude for cooking? Was he actually trying to make her feel better? My gosh, maybe she had made more progress with him last time than she thought! He actually seemed to care.

"Yes, you're right," she said. "I'll have to think about it some more and decide what I really want to do."

"What you should decide, Marla, is what your long-term goals are for your life. It's not good just to drift from one thing to another. You need to decide where you want to be ten years from now, twenty years from now, even thirty. Have you ever considered your future that way?"

Marla's eyes squinted slightly as she looked at him. She suddenly felt as if she were back in high school, talking to her career counselor. "Occasionally," she said, wondering where all this was coming from.

"What are some of your goals, then? Can you articulate them?" he asked, pausing to look at her seriously.

Can I articulate them, she repeated to herself. Jack had never talked like that before. What was going on here? "In twenty or thirty years I intend to be a successful businesswoman, running my own business. And I expect to be happily married," she said simply and with confidence.

Jack seemed to consider what she said and nodded. "That sounds very good."

Thanks, she thought ironically. She was glad he finally approved of something.

"But to reach those goals, you have to make plans and arrive at decisions carefully. And avoid mistakes," he said.

Avoid mistakes, she thought. Maybe now they were getting to the bottom of all this high-blown talk. "Mistakes?" she said.

He was quiet a moment as he worked, as if considering how to put what he was going to say next. "We all make mistakes, Marla . . ."

"Yes."

"Some mistakes can't be helped, and some—are because we don't stop to think, because we're emotional . . ."

"Because we act on impulse," she said.

"That's a good way to put it."

"And what impulsive mistakes have you made, Jack? I notice you used the plural *we.*"

He looked up at her abruptly, as if taken off-guard. "I . . ."

"Getting involved in an affair with me?"

He lowered his eyes. "Yes, I guess that was an impulsive mistake on my part. But we were talking about you," he said, his voice growing stern, almost parental.

"Well, I guess I made the same mistake as you," she said, a hint of anger in her tone. She resented him speaking only of *her* actions, as if he had had nothing to do with it.

"Yes, but our affair wasn't the only mistake you've made, was it?" he said.

"I don't imagine it was your only mistake, either," she countered.

"We're speaking about you right now, Marla." He sounded as if he was trying to keep his patience.

"Why? Why only me?"

"Because I want to. Because I care what happens to you, in spite of everything. You said you wanted to be friends, and I'm trying to be a friend to you. I think you need some direction in your life, and I'm hoping to help you sort things out, that's all," he said. His tone was soothing now, like a doctor's bedside manner.

Marla took a deep breath. *Oh, Lord,* she thought. She was beginning to understand now what he was doing, where he was coming from in this analytical discussion. He was seeing her objectively, she supposed, perhaps the way he had to look at anyone in order to paint him or her. But what exactly was he seeing? A flawed woman who needed his guidance? It didn't make sense. He had always said that she was strong and independent. Why did he think she needed his help? And why had he suddenly decided to be her *friend?*

"I see," she said, sounding ready to listen. "Exactly what sort of direction were you hoping to give me?"

"I want you to be the fine, prudent sort of woman I'm sure you're capable of being," he said.

"Prudent?"

"Well, be honest with yourself, Marla. You weren't very prudent in the way you behaved with me, were you?" he said gently. He set down his brush, as if to give her his full attention.

"Were you prudent with me?" she asked.

He gave a short sigh. "Marla, I think I understand myself better than you understand yourself." He gestured with his free hand. "I've accepted my own mistakes, I've learned from them, and I don't intend to repeat them. I don't think you've reached that stage yet. I want to help you realize that."

"Oh. Go on, then, and explain it to me," she said, sincerely interested, but not in the way he probably thought she was.

"All right. Let's try and see exactly how you've behaved,

65

just since I've known you. I can only guess how you were before we met." He paused, thoughtful. "You—became physically involved with me as easily as you might drink a glass of orange juice in the morning. Then you chased after Devin. And now, since I ended our affair, you see me as a conquest again. That's why you commissioned me to do this portrait, isn't it? To get me back? You said one of your goals was to be happily married. How can you expect to find happiness in marriage when you flit from one man to another? You have to try to overcome your wanderlust, Marla, and settle for one man, whoever he might be. You have to accept him, flaws and all, for the rest of your life. That's what marriage is."

Marla was having difficulty containing herself. "I'm glad you understand so well what marriage is," she said, "since you're the man I intend to marry." Just at the moment, though, she would be hard put to explain why.

Jack shook his head and set his wood palette down on the worktable. He half-sat, half-leaned on the table, giving her his undivided attention. "You only *think* you want to marry me," he said, his manner still clinical. "You got bored with me before and chased after another man. If you married me, you'd certainly get bored again." Resentment began to edge into his voice. "Frankly, Marla, I don't think you're ready to marry anyone yet. You like variety too much. You like the challenge of attracting a man's attention, and then once you've gotten it, you need the excitement of a new challenge. That's what you need to understand and work out for yourself. All I can do," he said, folding his arms across his chest, "is point it out and try to make you see it. I have no idea how to help you overcome it." His tone was dispassionate now, with a touch of self-righteousness that infuriated Marla.

"How dare—"

"Jack?" Claire said, knocking as she opened the door.

"Yes?"

66

"There's a customer downstairs asking about that landscape of the old farmhouse you did. He'd like to talk to you," Claire told him.

"Sure," Jack said and quickly walked out, leaving Marla alone and fuming. She got up and took a few agitated steps around the couch.

She knew he had come to look upon her as easy with men, but what he had just described was a nymphomaniac! Is that what he had convinced himself she was, in order to put her out of his mind? Making her out to be some neurotic man-chaser allowed him to feel guiltless, she supposed, the unsuspecting victim of her predatory ways.

The ego men had! Nothing that went wrong was ever *their* fault. Months ago, on that memorable second date, it was he who had suggested they go to bed. Just because she had gone along with the idea, why did that make *her* easy? Couldn't he be accused of the same?

Well, men never saw things that way, she reminded herself with a sigh. The point was that that was what he was telling himself. And by seeing her as a misguided sex addict, he had now managed to make himself feel good by being sorry for her. If she was no longer the healthy, normal woman he had fallen in love with, he could distance himself from her.

She was glad that Claire had interrupted them before she had a chance to blow up at him. This way she could pretend to play along while she thought about what to do next.

Marla had regained her composure when Jack came back into the room. "Did you make a sale?" she asked, taking her pose position again.

"Looks like it. He wants it reframed, though. Claire's seeing to it," Jack said. He picked up his brush and began to work.

"Good for Claire," Marla said under her breath. In a normal tone she said, "Well, you've given me a lot to think about, Jack—all those things you said about me and men and marriage."

He looked at her, concern in his eyes. "Have I? I hope so."

"Oh, yes. It's really kind of you to have thought so much about it in order to help me. I think you're right; I'm not ready for marriage."

The expression in his blue eyes changed slightly. There was an element of confusion in them now. "What do you think you'll do?" he asked, hesitant.

"I'm not sure. I'll have to take some time to think it through. I hope in the end I'll be able to become as self-controlled and morally responsible as you are," she said, trying her best to sound sincere. She looked at him steadily. "Sex can be a dangerous thing if it's misused." Her voice low and lilting, she spoke the words softly. She saw a small flame ignite in his eyes before he looked away. No, he wasn't nearly so self-disciplined as he thought he was. And Marla intended to prove it to him.

At the end of the week Marla reappeared at the gallery for her final sitting. She had had to take time off from work again, but she felt it was well worth it. She was wearing her usual long black skirt and white blouse. There was, however, one slight change in her attire: She had purposely left her bra in her dresser drawer at home. It wouldn't be too noticeable, she hoped. At least not at first. The white material of the blouse was opaque, but it was clingy enough to clearly reveal details to the observant eye.

Unfortunately it was Claire who had the observant eye. Upstairs in the studio, while Jack attended to his paints and brushes as usual, Claire's eyes kept drifting downward every few seconds as she spoke to Marla.

"How's—your cat?" she said.

Marla smiled, pretending nothing was different. "Oh, he's fine. I've made an appointment at the vet to have him neutered. I don't want him running around the neighborhood making all kinds of little cats when he's fully grown."

"N-no, I guess you wouldn't." Claire smiled nervously and cleared her throat. "I guess I'll get back to my book-keeping . . . unless you need me here for anything, Jack?"

"No. Thanks, Claire."

She walked out quietly, looking back once more at Marla before closing the door behind her.

"How are you today?" Marla said to Jack as she sat on the arm of the couch.

"Fine. How are you?"

"Well . . ." She purposely hesitated. "A little tired. I've had trouble sleeping. What we talked about last time has been playing on my mind, I'm afraid." It was true, but not in the way she was leading him to believe.

"Has it?" He was looking at her eyes. "You do look a little tired. I'm sorry."

"Oh, no, I . . . it's good for me. I need to think seriously about my life—and the way I've behaved." She bowed her head.

"Marla," he said, his tone very gentle, "you'll have to sit up and look at me. I can't paint you otherwise."

She did straighten and look up. It was then she saw him smiling, a sad smile, but still, a smile. He had never looked at her in quite that way before. It brought a slight glaze to her eyes.

His smile faded. "Marla . . ." He sounded worried, even apprehensive. "You aren't going to cry, are you?"

Yes, actually she was planning to—later. The caring look he had given her had made her unexpectedly emotional. "No," she said, blinking once. "I'm fine."

"Good. Now, head up high. That's it. Beautiful," he said.

She smiled and wished he would always be this way. He was probably assuming he would be parting with her today for the last time, and he wanted to be on good terms with her for his conscience's sake.

After several minutes of silence went by, she asked,

"What will you do with your future, Jack? Do you have any goals?"

"I'd like to expand the gallery eventually. I'd like to become a nationally known artist, too, I suppose," he said with a little grin.

"I'm sure you will be," she said. "And what about marriage? Do you hope to be married ten years from now?"

His expression clouded and his jaw muscles clenched. "Yes, I'd like to be married. If I can find the right woman."

"Of course," Marla said. "The right woman. What about Claire? She's available, she understands your work, and . . . I think she likes you." Marla smiled as she spoke, but she felt her stomach tightening at her own suggestion.

Jack looked up at her, his eyes wide and startled. The brush he was holding slipped out of his hand. He caught it as it fell onto the table beside him.

Marla laughed. "Looks like you hadn't thought about it."

"Obviously you have," he said tersely, working closely on the painting now.

Marla's heart rate increased. Was he upset that she had proposed he marry Claire, as if she no longer wanted him herself? She was almost sure her suggestion had wounded him.

She let him work in silence for about ten minutes, then said, "Jack, can I take a break now? I'm so tired today, it's hard to sit for long."

"Sure," he said and went on painting.

She walked over to the coffee maker. "Would you like some coffee? Claire's got it all ready. Cookies, too."

"Okay," he said absently.

She poured a cup and picked up a large oatmeal cookie to bring to him. "Can I see the portrait yet?" she asked as he took them from her.

"At the end of this session you can see it," he said.

"You're so disciplined. I've really come to appreciate the

70

value of that trait lately," she said, looking up at him with admiration.

He smiled and glanced away, looking a little self-conscious. But she could tell he liked her praise.

"I'm afraid I'm hopeless," she said, gazing forlornly at the floor.

"Now, Marla, nothing is impossible. You show a lot of discipline in your real estate work. You just need to apply that to the rest of your life."

"You mean—the men in my life," she said, slowly raising her fingertips to her breastbone. She glanced up and saw that his eye had followed the movement of her hand, as she had hoped. An absorbed look came into his eyes. He was finally noticing that she was wearing nothing beneath her blouse. She took a deep breath until, without looking, she could feel her nipples straining against the white material. "I never thought I had trouble saying no to men." She exhaled the long sigh she had been retaining for his benefit. "But you've made me see that I must have been deluding myself,"

He turned away to set the cup of coffee and partly eaten cookie on the table. "I think we'd better get back to work if we're going to finish today," he said tightly. He didn't look at her again.

She went quietly back to the couch and sat on the arm of it, though not in her proper pose. Instead, she slumped forward and covered her face with her hands.

"What's wrong?"

"Oh, nothing," she said, her voice muffled by her hands. "I . . . just . . ."

She heard his footsteps moving toward her. "What, Marla?" There was concern in his voice.

"I'm just . . . so upset . . . what you must think of me . . ." she said brokenly.

"Now, Marla, please . . ." She felt his comforting hand on her shoulder.

71

Leaning foward, she hooked her fingers over his belt, burying her face in his shirt.

"Marla, try to get hold of yourself. Come, sit down here." Grasping her by her upper arms, he made her rise, then sit down on the cushion of the couch. He sat next to her, one arm lightly over her shoulders. "You're not so bad as all that. Don't cry."

"I'm not?" she said sadly, taking her hands from her face and laying her head dejectedly against his shoulder. "But last time you said . . ."

"I know. I was just exaggerating to get my point across. You have a lot of fine qualities. You know I've always admired your energy and beauty and independence."

"No, you don't like my independent nature," she sniffed. "And you think I'm—l-loose with men. . . ."

"I didn't say it that way. . . ."

"You said I was easy with you," she said, her voice small and hurt.

"Well . . ."

"You asked me to sleep with you, and I just wanted to please you. . . ."

"I know, I know." He rubbed the back of her hand, which lay limply in her lap, with his fingertips. She ached to respond to his touch. "It was probably my fault as much as yours that we got involved too quickly," he said.

"I respect you, Jack. I know we probably won't be seeing each other after today, and I want to leave thinking that I have your good opinion, at least." She tilted her face up to his as she leaned her head against his shoulder, bringing her mouth within range of his, but she made no further move.

"Of course you do," he said softly. As he looked at her face, changing emotions passed through his clear blue eyes—sadness, longing, weakening resistance. "You're so lovely. . . ." The words were almost incoherent. Slowly his lips drew near, pausing about an inch from hers. She could feel his uneven, warm breath on her cheek and chin. As if allowing himself one last fleeting taste of sweetness, he brushed her mouth lightly. But she leaned forward imperceptibly and made the kiss last longer than she knew he intended. He drew away from the heat of her mouth, his eyes flaming, luminous with desire as he looked at her. "Oh, Marla," he whispered. All at once he brought his lips to hers in a violent kiss, his last shred of restraint broken, all emotion finally unleashed. His strong arm about her shoulders gathered her to him while she raised her arms about his neck.

A small sound of joy escaped her throat as he crushed her against him. Oh, God, she had won! They were in each other's arms again, enfolded in passion, wanting each other desperately, just as it used to be. She needed him; she needed his love. She showed it in her kiss, giving and taking, opening her mouth to him while she coiled her fingers through his hair. "Jack, I need you, I need you," she said, her voice soft and husky. "I've missed you so terribly."

"I want you, Marla." His voice was thick, almost drunken with desire. "I want you so badly." His hand moved roughly over her breasts, feeling out her soft curves through her blouse. Fingers shaking, he tried to undo the small pearl buttons. When he couldn't manage it, he simply ripped her blouse open, exposing her white, rounded breasts and small, rose nipples. With a gentle hand he cupped one breast, toying with its tender weight, then caressing it with adoring care.

Marla gasped at the wondrous sensation only his touch could bring. Her breathing quickened and her heart pounded with deepening desire. "Oh, Jack," she said in a small voice, her vulnerability genuine this time.

His hand moved to her other breast, caressing it as he bent his head to kiss her slender neck. She moaned softly at the feel of his hot moist lips and his rough mustache on her tender skin. A warm shiver went through her with each kiss as he moved downward until he reached her nipple, erect with expectation. "Oh . . . Jack . . ." she moaned, her voice begging for more as she felt his tongue stimulate the small nub, giving her exquisite pleasure.

She undid the buttons of his shirt frantically, pushing her hands beneath to run her fingers through the matting of light brown chest hair. When she found his nipple, she bent forward to do for him what he had so expertly done for her. She felt his shiver of delight and noted with heady satisfaction how heavy and ragged his breathing was becoming.

He began pushing her downward, beneath him, onto the couch, until her head rested against the arm of it. Bringing his head to her chest, he kissed the hollow between her breasts while his fingers roved over the waistband of her skirt, urgently looking for the fastening.

"How do you get this damn thing off?" he said, looming over her now, his eyes afire and impatient.

Marla swallowed, trying desperately to control her own fires. This wasn't going quite as she had planned anymore. Without thinking, she took a breath to clear her head. It made her bared breasts rise invitingly toward him. He bent low over her to take her nipple again, licking and teasing it until she thought she would lose her mind.

Neither heard the knock, the soft voice, or the sound of the door opening. All Marla ever knew was that suddenly Claire was standing a few feet away, watching them in absolute shock.

"Jack," Marla said, trying to stop him, ". . . Claire . . ."

Jack lifted his head from Marla's swollen breast and pink, wet nipple to look first at her and then at Claire.

Claire was beginning to step backward. "I—excuse me." She turned and hurried from the room.

Jack ran a hand through his hair as if trying to bring himself back to reality. Then he gradually grew white with rage.

"Damn you!" he said hoarsely as Marla tried to sit up and cover herself. "You little slut!"

"How dare you say that!" she cried, deeply incensed at his calling her names when he had been willingly loving her a moment before. "You made all the moves! How dare you accuse me!"

"You seduced me into this. You made me want you again. I vowed to stay away from you, but you managed it again, didn't you, you witch! All that weeping and getting me to comfort you!" His voice was rough and bitter, his eyes wild with anger and desire.

Marla drew a breath to try to calm herself. "Well, we've proved one thing. You can't control yourself any better than you think I can. You accuse me of being easy—look at you!"

He got off the couch and paced a few vigorous but unstable steps. "You came here with this whole thing premeditated," he said, pointing his finger at her. "You tricked me into doing your portrait, and then you planned how to draw me into your web, just like a spider!" He waved his arms about as he spoke, indignance displayed in every gesture. "And me, the unsuspecting fly, fell closer and closer until I got caught in your trap!"

She could almost laugh at his pompous posturing, if she wasn't so outraged.

"My mother wanted a portrait for Christmas," she told him. "You can call and ask her, if you like, to see that it's true. And how did I seduce you? I came here, dressed from neck to toe, and all I did was sit on this couch hour after hour. You didn't have to come over here and rip apart my blouse! That was all your idea, Mr. Smug and Self-Righteous!" She spat the words at him, angry to the core. So what if she had planned the whole thing? It wasn't her fault he had cooperated so easily!

"It doesn't matter what you wore or what you did. You just have some kind of power over men. And don't you love to use it!" He blustered at her, his shirt still open, his chest

75

heaving with his heavy breathing. "You might as well have come here all gussied up like a harlot! Your intentions would have been exactly the same!"

She felt as if he had slapped her in the face. Her mouth trembled. "You'll regret you ever said that to me! I don't know why I should still love you, when all you do is abuse me and say mean things. I always thought I was pretty smart, but I guess I'm not. And you aren't either, Jack. We could be happy together if you would only let us." She stared at him, new resolve forming in her eyes. "But I haven't given up yet. And, what's more, you don't *want* me to give up. You still love me whether you admit it or not!" She turned then, head high, and walked out.

Jack stood where he was, speechless now. He had heard everything she told him, but only one thing she had said kept whirling through his mind: *I don't know why I should still love you.* She had never used that word before: *love.*

CHAPTER FIVE

Jack stood in front of Marla's portrait for some time after she had stalked out. He didn't know how long. His body was still cooling down from the heated passions that had inflamed him when she was in his arms. It had shaken him to realize he still craved her so desperately. How she had responded to his kisses! Did she love him? Should he trust her? He needed her. Even now he could still feel the force of life flowing through his veins from those moments in her embrace. He was only half alive without her.

But half alive was better than the decimation he would feel if he trusted her and she went off to another man again. She had explained all her reasons for flirting with Devin. But how could Jack know for sure they weren't just excuses she had invented? She was so clever. Look at how he had gotten involved with her again, even though he had had his guard up! It was all just a physical fascination for her, anyway. He ought to be able to rise above his sexual hunger for a woman he couldn't respect and no longer loved. If he didn't, he'd always be a prey to her wiles.

"E-excuse me—Jack?" It was Claire's very self-conscious voice. She was standing in the doorway Marla had left open.

Jack turned to her, then, remembering what she had seen, felt himself blush deeply. He couldn't think of a thing to say.

"I—just wanted to apologize for interrupting the way I did," she said haltingly. She cast her eyes this way and that about the room, apparently too embarrassed to look at him.

"A customer was asking about a painting that had no price tag, so . . ." Her voice faded off in confusion.

Though Jack suspected he was three times as mortified as she was, he nevertheless felt sorry for her. The situation in which she found herself was very awkward, especially for a woman like Claire. He had to give her credit for having the strength of character to come up and apologize.

"No, it's not your fault at all," he told her. "In fact, I'm glad you came in when you did." His voice was tinged with bitterness.

"You are? Oh—you mean you were in a "—she seemed to be searching for the proper words—"a situation that you didn't intend to find yourself in?"

He raised his brows at her perception. "Yes, that's it exactly, Claire. It's I who should apologize to you for allowing such a—a situation, as you put it, to happen here, where we both are supposed to be working."

"Oh, please don't say that," Claire said sincerely, looking at him now. She took a few steps toward him. "I'm sure it wasn't your fault."

"You're—very understanding," he said. He felt a twinge of conscience, though he didn't know why he should. It *wasn't* his fault.

"Well, if I may speak frankly . . ." Claire said.

"Please do."

"I suspected that just such a thing might happen with—with that woman. Intuition told me she's a man-chaser, and she's after you. I was afraid, being so intent on your work, you might not realize it."

Jack could have laughed. Of course he realized it. He knew Claire had her sights on him, too. Lately he'd begun to feel like the fox in a hunt. "You think she's a man-chaser?" He was curious about Claire's perception of Marla.

"I would say so. She's very pretty, of course, but she has that seductive sort of look about her. Just consider how she was flaunting herself at you—her blouse all undone, shame-

78

lessly using her body to entice you. In my book, she's nothing more than a tramp."

Tramp. Jack had called Marla worse things himself. But, to his surprise, he felt anger begin to rise in him. His chest constricted to repress it and he stiffened.

"I really don't understand how a woman can lower herself to behave like that," Claire went on. "No pride whatsoever. I'm sorry a man of your refinement had to be exposed to such a vulgar female."

Suddenly Jack had heard enough. He turned on her sharply. "Be quiet!" he said in a low, tightly controlled voice. "I won't hear anything said against her! Marla's a beautiful woman with a passionate nature, who isn't afraid of life. I admire her! And what happened here today was as much my doing as hers."

Claire was scanning his face incredulously. She seemed at a loss for a moment, then said, "I . . . sorry. Perhaps I should go downstairs in case another customer comes."

She walked out quietly, leaving Jack with the upsetting realization that he still loved Marla very deeply.

Late that afternoon Jack was getting ready to close the gallery. Claire had just left. They had spoken to each other a few times during the afternoon about business matters. His sharp words to her earlier were apparently put aside, and things seemed to be back to normal between them. It was good to have something normal.

As for Marla, Jack didn't know what to think. He only knew he loved her and he wanted to believe she truly loved him. But he was still afraid to believe it, and he didn't know what his next step with her should be. Meanwhile her nearly finished portrait waited in his studio.

The phone rang. Somehow he knew before he picked it up who it would be. "Hello?"

"It's Marla. I'm wondering what we should do about the painting. Is it finished?" Her tone was curt.

He copied her manner. "It still needs a little work. You left before the sitting was over."

"What do you suggest we do about it?"

"What do *you* suggest?" he said. He knew she must have something in mind.

"I'd like to get it over with, as I'm sure you would," she replied. "If you're not busy, why don't I come over tonight and finish posing? I'll have the check ready to pay you for the portrait."

My, she was businesslike, he thought. He couldn't help but smile a little. What was she planning this time? "That's fine with me," he said, keeping his voice crisp.

"After dinner, about seven?" she said.

"Okay."

Jack found himself watching out the window for her when seven o'clock came. Soon her white car pulled up in front of the gallery. He unlocked the front door and let her in. She was wearing her long black skirt, but a different blouse. The style was similar to the one she had worn before, but the color was deep blue.

"Sorry," she said coolly when she saw him eyeing her clothes. "The other blouse needs mending. I don't think I need to remind you why. This was the next best thing I could find."

"It's all right," he said. "Shall we go up?"

He followed her up the staircase, his pulses keen with just-below-the-surface excitement. Marla always did that to him, whether he liked it or not. Tonight he had to admit he was looking forward to being within range of her mysterious gravitational pull, whatever came of it.

He turned on the bright ceiling lights he had had installed so he could work after dark. Marla took her usual pose on the couch, her posture stately, her head high, her expression confident and composed. He studied her as he slowly walked to the easel. God, she was regal tonight. What was that line from the *Song of Songs? Who is she that looketh forth as the morning, fair as the moon, clear as the sun, and terrible as an army with banners?* He had always liked the poetic language of those ancient words, though he never could figure out what they meant. Looking at Marla now, he felt he finally understood.

Picking up his palette, he began to mix colors on it. Mainly he had a few details to polish on her face and hair, and some work on the background.

After several minutes he was beginning to grow uncomfortable with her icy silence until, all at once, she broke it. "Have you found some plausible way to explain to yourself why you tried to make love to me this afternoon?" she said, her tone sure and cutting.

"We were once lovers," he said calmly, working as he talked. "It's not unusual for an old attraction to flare up on occasion. It doesn't necessarily mean anything."

"Ah," she said. "So at least you aren't accusing me of seducing you anymore."

"I didn't say that. I think your whole intention in having me paint your portrait was to seduce me. But I admit I was probably willing to be seduced, though I didn't realize it."

"No, you were too busy trying to get my wayward soul back on the straight and narrow path," she said.

Jack smiled at the remark, tacitly admitting his own foolishness, but he said nothing.

"I'm anxious to see the portrait," she said, after a moment. "Have you painted in a scarlet letter on my blouse? Do I have a broom and a boiling cauldron?"

Jack grinned slightly to himself. "Come and look at it, if you like."

She seemed surprised. "Now?"

He nodded. "I just have a little to finish on the background. I don't think I need you to pose anymore."

She walked slowly toward the easel, as if almost afraid to look. As she came around it to stand next to him, he felt his senses heighten at her nearness. He could smell her perfume. He longed to caress her silky hair. But he made no move.

Marla looked at the portrait for several long moments in absolute silence. He began to wonder if she liked it.

Finally she swallowed, and in a voice much less firm than before she said, "I'm—at a loss." She smiled, but her lips trembled slightly. "You've made me much more beautiful than I am."

He wanted to say *No, I haven't*, but kept himself from doing so. He thought he had only barely captured her vibrance and loveliness.

"Thank you," she said softly. "It's wonderful."

He nodded, acknowledging her compliment, then stepped away from her a bit. If he had remained as close to her as he was, he'd have her in his arms again in a moment, and he wasn't sure that was wise.

She was staring up at him now, as if she knew why he had edged away. "You know what I think, Jack?" Her voice had confidence again. "I think you painted me this way because you still love me." Her large, lustrous brown eyes remained steadily on him, challenging him to deny it.

"You think so?" he said lightly, putting down his brush and palette to wipe his hands on a rag. His hands were clean, but he needed to do something, and he was too confused at the moment to continue to paint.

"Yes," she said.

"Well, we're all entitled to our opinions."

Her eyes showed momentary disappointment. She walked away from him, back toward the couch. But he suspected she wasn't finished with him yet.

She stopped in front of the couch, her back to him. "I was wondering if you would do another portrait of me, Jack," she said, speaking over her shoulder to him.

The suggestion took him by surprise. "Another one?"

"Yes," she said. "This one you've done is beautiful, almost too perfect." Her back was still to him and she seemed to be fidgeting with her clothes, but he wasn't sure. "I'd like to have one done that shows me the way *you* see me," she said, "so I can see myself that way." His eyes widened. She was taking off her blouse. "I thought maybe this outfit might be suitable," she said as she tossed her blouse aside. She turned to face him, then unfastened her skirt and let it fall to her feet.

She was wearing an old-fashioned red satin corset, trimmed with black lace over her breasts. A black lace ruffle decorated the bottom of the tight garment at her hips and stomach, just beneath her cinched waist. Below were black garter straps, which hooked into and held up black lace stockings. Last, and least, was a filmy black bikini panty that barely covered what it was meant to cover.

Jack felt as if the breath had been knocked out of him. Then, as she moved toward him, he felt an undeniable surge of pure lust. She was the sexiest woman he had ever seen.

As she moved closer, his desire only became more acute. She stopped about three feet away from him. Hands at her tiny waist, she shifted her weight onto one dainty high-heeled foot, making her hips swing provocatively. Her slender, bared thighs were accented by the black stockings that ended several inches above her shapely knees. Her breasts were pushed up by the stiff corset, exaggerating her soft white cleavage. He could just see the hint of her nipples through the black lace. He wanted to kiss her and bite her and whisper sexy things in her ear. Most of all he wanted to tug down those wispy panties, be within her and experience all her warm, life-giving femininity.

"Where did you get that?" he said, resentful because she had made him so vulnerable again, angry with himself because he wanted her so badly.

"I took a run up to a little shop in Seattle," she said. "Like it?"

"No!"

"You said this afternoon that I might as well have come

83

all gussied up like a—I won't repeat the word you used. Anyway, here I am." She stepped closer, then pressed her body lightly against his, just touching him, especially below the waist. "You like it, Jack," she whispered provocatively. "I can tell."

Jack clenched his jaw. "All right," he said quietly. Within him a battle was raging, an intense struggle with himself to quell his overpowering desire. "I like it. Any normal man would. You came here dressed like this knowing I would respond. It's just another of your plans to break my resistance."

She smiled, her eyes alight with humor. "Yes, it is," she freely admitted. "Maybe I'm everything you've said I am. Maybe I'm easy, maybe I have tried to seduce you. Maybe I'm just plain naughty." She ran her hand slowly up his shirt. "But I think you love me no matter what you imagine I am. Even if I were the most scandalous woman in the world, you would still want me."

Jack stared at her, eyes burning. He could feel his heart pounding and the blood pulsating hotly through his veins. "All right, I want you. Yes, damn it, I want you!" Reaching for her, he caught her to him in a shattering kiss. He wished he could break her, but he couldn't destroy the thing he loved. Tears rose to his eyes with an emotion so strong it was overwhelming.

He smothered her with his deep kiss until he could feel her growing lax in his arms. Feverishly he kissed her neck and then the alluring swells of her breasts above the lace. His hands moved down to her rounded buttocks. Slipping his fingers beneath the panties, he squeezed her flesh and pressed her urgently against his pelvis, wanting to bury himself in her softness. "Marla," he groaned, beside himself with need.

Picking her up in his arms, he carried her to the couch. "Jack," she protested limply as he placed her on it. She put up her arms as if to protect herself from his forcefulness.

Thinking that in his frenzy for her he might be frightening her, he reined in his passion a bit and tried to move more slowly. It was a monumental sacrifice; he wanted desperately to possess her.

Her hands were pushing against his chest, but he slowly eased himself down on top of her, and she gave way to him as their lips met. He buried his fingers in her thick hair as his tongue entwined with hers. His hot mouth moved down her chin, then to her long, slender throat, kissing every inch, tasting her delicate skin. When he reached her breast, he pushed down the black lace to capture her bared nipple between his lips. He stimulated the pert little nub with his tongue until she softly moaned with need, then bit it lightly with his teeth, making her gasp.

Her sensual sounds only excited him more. He was at his limit now. Hands trembling, he reached below to her panties. There was no time to undress, but it didn't matter. He wanted to love her just like this, black lace, red satin and all.

He was tugging at her panties when it seemed as if she suddenly awoke from her sensual daze. "Jack," she said, fighting his hands at her hips. "No!"

"What do you mean?"

"I won't make love with you like this," she said, her voice uneven and breathless.

"Why not?" he asked, astonished.

"You'll have to marry me first."

He couldn't believe what she was saying. "What!" He pushed himself away from her slightly and stared down at her, eyes blazing.

"You said yourself our affair was a big mistake and you didn't want to repeat it." She spoke in a rush of words. "I want to be married to you before we make love again, so that you'll be sure of my intentions and my commitment. You see, Jack," she said, edging herself out from under him, "I'm not so easy as you think. I *can* say no, though I want you more than anything right now."

85

Jack was furious. They had reached this height of passion, and she was going to refuse? Hold out for marriage? "You conniving tart!" He loomed toward her as she huddled against the edge of the couch. "You bring me to this in order to wheedle a marriage license out of me!" He swore and then pushed himself off the sofa. "You think I would marry you, especially after this piece of trickery? You think I'd want a wife who never does anything honestly if she can do it through manipulation? I wouldn't do business with a person like you, much less marry you!"

"I had to do this," she protested. "Trying to talk to you honestly got me nowhere. You're like a mule—the only way to get your attention is to hit you between the eyes with a two-by-four!"

"I might have preferred that to sexual baiting!" he said, aching with frustration. His body surged with a need that wouldn't be satisfied now because of her game playing.

Her eyes softened. "Do you want me, Jack? Just say you'll marry me, and I'll gladly make love with you now. I want to, too."

He was sorely tempted, but his head was clear enough not to fall for a trap like that. "Sexual blackmail! I won't be ramrodded into anything. I've had enough of your scheming."

"We could be happy married to each other," she said, her voice taking on a pleading quality. "I'm sure we could. You want me and I want you. We've just proved that. You've tried all this time to convince yourself that you don't love me, but you still do. Why don't we just get married and stop all this nonsense?"

"Nonsense is right!" he railed at her, quickly pacing back and forth in front of her. "I *couldn't* love someone like you. And even if I did, I wouldn't be stupid enough to marry you!"

She looked stricken. "Don't say that, Jack," Marla begged

in a voice hushed with emotion. "You do love me. Look at the beautiful way you painted me. You must love me."

"I'm fascinated by you—entranced, bewitched. I'm ashamed to admit how weak I am, how confused and disoriented I get when I'm around you. But for once I'm thinking clearly! You've added the straw that broke the camel's back, Marla. I'd never marry you after the way you tried to use me tonight. That beauty of yours that's kept me wanting you is only skin deep. What's beneath isn't so pretty." He walked over to where her skirt had fallen to the floor. Picking up the black bundle of taffeta, he tossed it over her as she sat on the couch. "Take your trollop's garb and get out of here. Go on, get out!" He pointed toward the door, eyes smoldering with rage.

She looked hopelessly crestfallen, as if she had played her last card and lost all she had. "Jack, please . . ." she said brokenly.

"Get out!" he yelled. *"Tramp!"*

Clutching her skirt, she ran out of the room. He heard her footsteps down the stairs, and then his front door slammed shut. With the sound of her car motor disappearing in the distance, he knew she was out of his life.

Jack paced about the room for some time, making resolute gestures as he silently spoke to himself, assuring himself he was right to be angry and that he was glad she was gone. But within an hour he felt empty and forlorn, exactly the way Marla looked when she ran from the room. The remaining ache of unrequited sexual need had ebbed away, leaving a cold, desolate feeling in his body.

Why did he want her so much? Why Marla in particular of all the women he'd ever met? Why would no other suit him? Did he have to spend the rest of his life alone because she had spoiled him for anyone else?

The thought of continuing his present lonely life made him bow his head. He sank down onto the couch. Why did he have to love her? She was beautiful and spirited, a rare woman to appear in any man's life. But he had told her himself her beauty was only skin deep. Look at her trickery wearing that gaudy corset under her blouse and skirt! The image of her in the risqué undergarments formed before his eyes and gave him a renewed surge of longing. He shouldn't be so weak, such a prey to her sexual manipulation. If he could make himself see her as an unscrupulous woman given to outlandish schemes, maybe he could forget her. What she'd done tonight *was* ridiculous. Imagine, she'd driven all the way to Seattle to find that corset, then called and come over to finish the pose, all the while planning to reveal her sexy costume to him. And then when she'd gotten him out of his head with desire, she'd said, *You'll have to marry me first!* If it had happened to someone else, he would be laughing at the story.

Jack smiled wistfully. Yes, Marla was quite a woman. Maybe he was taking her premeditation too seriously. She'd told him she wasn't going to let him go, but he never imagined she would be so inventive and determined—all for him. Maybe she did love him. No one else had ever gone to such lengths to claim him. If he married Marla, life would never be dull, that was for sure.

If he married her. Was he foolish to consider it? Yes, she was lovely, responsive, scintillating—everything that made his pulses race and made him feel alive. But what was most important in the end—to have a gorgeous temptress who excited him, or a woman he could trust? Or was he thinking now he might have both in Marla? If it was true that she loved him, could he trust her?

Tramp! The word echoed again and again in Marla's ears. The man she loved had called her that and more. And what was worse, she deserved it.

She curled her legs up closer as she sat on her living room couch early Sunday afternoon. It was well past noon, but she was still wearing her long pale blue terry cloth robe over her nightgown. She hadn't seen any purpose in getting dressed. Yesterday at the office she had been miserable trying to work. Instead of properties and buyers, all she could think about was Jack. Today she had decided just to take the day off and stay home, even if it was Sunday, a busy day for the real estate business. She had to pull herself together somehow. But she didn't know how.

Tears came to her reddened eyes once again, and she pulled out her damp handkerchief from the robe's pocket. She had to stop this crying. It wasn't at all like her to weep hour after hour. She had never been emotional. Lately tears had seemed to come easily, but she was always able to control them. Today, though, she was simply falling apart.

Well, it was her own fault she had come to this. She should have known playing the temptress with Jack would only make things worse. She had hoped to make him realize that he still wanted her in spite of everything. But all it had done was prove to him that she was exactly what he had decided she was—easy, scheming and all those other things he had called her.

Her cat jumped on the couch and nuzzled against her arm, then climbed onto her lap. "Hi, Maxie," she said, sniffing, then smiling a bit. A loud purr started as she ran her hand along the soft fur of his back. It seemed Max was the only living thing around to console her. She hadn't yet told Ginger and Devin that she had lost Jack for good. She just hadn't felt up to phoning them. But it was probable that Ginger would call her next week to meet for lunch. Marla hoped she would be able to relate her final defeat with some amount of dignity.

She felt she had lost all self-respect, knowing what Jack would always think of her. How humiliated and bewildered she had been when she ran from his studio, still dressed in her red corset and black lace stockings. She had thought she had him in the palm of her hand. But his poor opinion of her was so strong, it had transcended everything, even his strong sexual desire, and left her figuratively in the gutter—where he no doubt thought she belonged. She had underestimated him and the strength of his resolve. He simply didn't want her to be his wife anymore, and that was that. And that meant he didn't love her anymore, either, or else he would have found it in his heart to forgive her shortcomings.

And what was there to do now? she asked herself, picking up Max and holding the cat in her arms. Continue as before, she supposed. But she no longer wanted to go on as before. She was growing tired of living alone and tired of her job as well. It was difficult enough to change careers in midstream, but it was even harder to decide you didn't want to be single anymore when there was no available man around. She didn't want any man but Jack anyway.

Maybe she shouldn't give up yet. Maybe there was some other approach she could try. She knew she would have to see Jack once more to pick up the painting and give him her check. There must be something she could say or do . . .

Why think that? she asked herself as new tears rose in her eyes. He'd never listen to a thing she said, not after the way he had thrown her out. And Claire would probably deliver the painting. Jack wouldn't take any chance on actually seeing her. Tomorrow she'd probably get a call from Claire, asking in her ladylike voice when it would be convenient to bring the portrait to her. How mortifying to have to see that immaculate goody-two-shoes again after all that had happened. Claire, in her demure afternoon-tea outfits and with her perfect manners . . .

The doorbell rang, interrupting her thoughts. "Oh, no," Marla said. The last thing she wanted was to see anyone. She stayed where she was, holding Max on her lap, and decided not to answer it. After a few moments the bell rang again, making the cat skittish. In several more seconds it rang a third time. Marla stood up with Max in her arms and tried to peek out the front window, but her view was limited and she couldn't see anyone. She decided it was probably a neighborhood kid selling raffle tickets or something. Maybe she should just buy whatever he had and send him on.

Holding Max in one arm, she opened the door. She was shocked when she saw Jack standing before her. Instantly she turned pale. He was dressed in a shirt, a tan pullover sweater and dark blue pants. Beside him he was holding a large, thin, rectangular package wrapped in brown paper. Max, still fearful of any human he didn't know, jumped over her shoulder to the floor and fled into the kitchen, though Marla barely noticed as she gaped at Jack.

"What was that?" Jack asked. His expression seemed calm as he looked at her.

"What? Oh—m-my cat."

"Friendly pet you've got there," he said dryly. "I called your office—I thought you'd be working today. They said you took the day off. I'm glad to find you home."

Marla stared at him in whirling confusion and said nothing.

"May I come in?"

Her eyes and brain focused slightly. "You want to come in?"

"If you don't mind," he said.

"No, n-not—I don't—not at all." She didn't even know what she'd said as she stood aside to let him in. As she closed the door, she happened to glance down at her robe and was suddenly aware of how awful she must look. *Oh, Lord,* she thought, running her fingers through her uncombed hair. Why was he here?

"Here's your painting, all finished," he said, leaning it against an easy chair. "It's still not quite dry, but it's framed and ready to hang. I wrapped it loosely, so be careful when you unwrap the paper not to touch the paint."

"All right," Marla said, finally beginning to collect herself. So that was why he had come. At least he hadn't sent Claire. "It was nice of you to bring it over. I'll get you the check. It's in my purse." She began to walk to her bedroom door.

"Don't bother," he said.

She turned. "Don't . . . ? Well, I have to pay you for it."

"No."

Marla was all confused again. "I—don't understand."

Jack glanced downward for an instant. "I came over mainly to talk to you," he said. "Not to deliver the painting."

"Oh." Talk? About what? Her heartbeat seemed to become irregular for a moment. "But it'll only take a second to get you the check." She moved toward the door again, hurrying, not so much to get the check anymore as to comb her hair at her bedroom mirror, so he wouldn't have to continue to look at her frazzled appearance.

"Marla."

She was at the door. "Back in a second."

"Marla!" His voice stopped her just as she was about to escape into her room. "Never mind the check. Come here."

She obeyed, a fretful look on her face. "I have to insist on paying you for the portrait," she said when she came up to him. However bedraggled and sad she might look, she didn't want the painting as a gift because he now felt sorry for her.

"I don't think it'll be appropriate after you hear what I have to say." Standing close, she could see he was growing a trifle nervous. "Will you—sit down with me?" he asked, motioning toward her white couch.

Tightness gripped her stomach and throat. What was he going to say? She nodded and walked with him to the sofa, then sat down a little distance from him. "What did you want to tell me?" she asked, apprehensive, half afraid he was going to make some more comments about her outrageous behavior. She didn't know if she could take any more condemnation, or even his polite apology for having thrown her out, if that was what he intended.

"First, I wanted to say I'm sorry for the way I spoke to you Friday night."

He was sitting forward in his seat instead of leaning back. He seemed stiff and mannered now. His blond hair must have been freshly washed, for it was light and soft-looking as it casually sloped to one side over his forehead, at odds with his rigid demeanor. She might have thought that he had taken special care with his appearance before coming over, for his clothes all looked neat and new, but why would he have bothered, just for her? Maybe he had some other appointment after stopping to see her.

"Are you listening to me?" he asked, narrowing his eyes to look at her as she sat studying him. "I said I apologize for the things I said."

"Y-yes, I heard. Thank you." So this was the real reason he had come. Well, it was kind of him, but she didn't want to hear it.

"I was angry . . ."

"I understand."

"Because I felt tricked," he continued.

Marla nodded. "Yes, I know."

"I was also frustrated—sexually, I mean."

"Yes . . ."

"I felt that you were preying on my weaknesses and—"

"You don't have to explain," she said.

"I want to explain!" he snapped. "Can't you be quiet and listen?"

"All right," she said acquiescently. Did she really have to hear all this? She supposed it was her just punishment for what she had put him through, but it was painful.

"I was angry," he repeated. "But later I realized it was more at myself than at you. I didn't want to think that I was such a—a pushover for you." His expression had an odd combination of humor and impatience. The more she studied him, the more Marla thought he was in a strange frame of mind.

93

He paused for a moment, as if immersed in his own thoughts. He ran a finger over his long, blondish brown mustache. "I was thinking about it all night Friday and all day yesterday. I decided, why shouldn't I be a pushover? You looked so good in that outfit, I wouldn't be a man if I didn't lose my head. And then I got to thinking how much trouble you had gone to, ever since we broke up, to invent ways to see me and to win me back. It's pretty flattering. I began to think that you must really . . . you must care for me a lot to have done all that." He glanced at her as if to see how she was reacting to what he was saying.

Marla felt as if her pulse and her senses had all stopped. She sat there looking at him, wide-eyed and pale. She swallowed. Was she hearing all this right? Did she have another chance? "Of course I care," she said in a heartfelt whisper.

He looked forward again. "The other day you said . . . that you loved me."

"I do, Jack. I do." She put shaking fingers out to touch his sleeve, trying to assure him in whatever way she could.

He looked at her again, eyes guarded. "You're sure?"

"Yes, absolutely sure! Ever since I l-lost you I've been sure." Tears filled her eyes.

His body seemed to relax, and he smiled. "I guess I can believe you," he said. "God, your eyes are beautiful with tears in them."

"How can you say that?" she said, reaching for her handkerchief. "I look awful today."

He laughed softly. "You never look awful. You couldn't. Your coloring and bone structure won't allow it. Not to mention that smashing, slinky body that I can never resist, try as I have."

Marla smiled and sniffed, her face brightening for the first time. "You did pretty well at resisting me."

"I won a few battles but lost the war," he murmured as if amused. His expression grew serious after a moment. He gazed at her solemnly. "I've tried my best to convince myself

94

that I can get along without you, that I don't want you, but it doesn't work. I love you, Marla. I love you dearly. I can't fight it anymore and . . . I'm willing to entrust my love to you, if you want it."

Eyes wide and wet, all Marla could do was stare at Jack in astonishment and nod her head.

"But"—there was a gentle warning in his voice and clear eyes—"I don't want you to take my love unless you're sure you can protect it and return it, and not for just a few weeks or a few months, but for always. If you're my wife, I expect you to behave, to keep yourself only for me and not look elsewhere. Do you hear?" His tone was very soft and low, but firm. Frighteningly firm.

"I hear." Her voice was only a whisper, but it carried all the sincerity of her heart. "I love you and I'll never want anyone else, Jack. You can trust me, I promise. I want more than anything to be your wife."

He smiled, his eyes full of love and pride. "That's all I want, too, darling." He took her warmly in his arms, hugging her to him.

Marla held him tightly as tears of joy slid down her cheeks. She was delirious with happiness. Suddenly everything had fallen into place—Jack had come back, he loved and wanted her, he was going to marry her! As she raised her face to his to kiss him, she made a vow to herself that she would never disappoint him again. Never.

CHAPTER SIX

"Are these supposed to be scrambled or sunny-side up?" Jack asked. He looked curiously at the plate Marla had just set in front of him.

"Sunny-side up," Marla said, sitting down across from him at the small breakfast table.

"They just got a little mixed up on their way to the frying pan?" He poked at the eggs with his fork.

"If you want eggs that are perfectly cooked, Jack," she said sweetly, "you know what you can do."

"Make them myself?"

"You got it."

He nodded. "This looks delicious!" he said with newfound enthusiasm.

She smiled. "I thought so."

They had been married exactly a week. It had been a small, very informal ceremony a few weeks after he had come to her house that Sunday afternoon. They had moved into his white wood-frame home then, located about two blocks from his gallery on the same street. They were sitting in the breakfast nook off the kitchen. It was situated in a bay window that looked out onto the large backyard garden. Jack had it kept in beautiful order by a local gardener.

Marla adored Jack's comfortable twenty-year-old home with its spacious rooms and didn't mind moving from her own house at all. In fact, she had just put her place up for sale. She loved being married, too. But that didn't prevent her from beginning her marriage as she intended to go on. She wasn't going to pretend to like chores she hated just to please her new husband. She might have briefly feigned an interest in cooking when Claire had seemed to be a threat, but that had only backfired anyway.

"Maybe we should buy a barbeque," she said as she adjusted her napkin in her lap. A large diamond gleamed from her left hand. She was dressed for work in a tan skirt and coordinated, colorful blouse.

Jack's brows raised in obvious surprise. "I didn't think you'd be interested in getting something like that."

She grinned a little. "I imagine you'd like it."

"Me? Well, yes, I like charcoal-broiled food. But why would *you* want one?"

"Because wherever I've been, it's always the man of the house who does the cooking on the outdoor grill," she said simply.

Jack chuckled. "I should have figured that one out. Okay, we can buy one."

It was Marla's turn to be surprised at his quick agreement. At that point Max jumped up onto the table and began to sniff at Jack's plate. In a fraction of a second the cat had made off with a strip of bacon.

"Maxie!" Marla said, laughing. She watched as her pet jumped off the table and began to eat the bacon on the ceramic-tiled floor.

"You'll never discipline him that way, Marla. You should swat him whenever he jumps on the table or the kitchen counter. Then we might live in the hope of not losing half of each meal to him," he said dryly.

Marla gave Jack a strip of bacon from her own plate. "I can't hit him," she said. "He moves too fast. Besides, everyone knows you can't train a cat. They're too independent."

"Cats and women," Jack muttered.

"What?"

"You're too lenient. You should train a pet to live under *your* rules. You shouldn't adapt your life to the animal."

Marla sighed. "Well, since you're so tough, you train him."

"He's not my cat," Jack said, making a disavowing gesture. "You brought him here, fleas and all."

"I comb him every day now. I rarely find a flea anymore. And don't say he's not your cat. You enjoy playing with him."

Jack's shoulders shook slightly with laughter. "Only when I don't mind getting tooth marks and scratches all over me! And why does he have to sleep on the bed with us?"

Marla shrugged. "I don't know. Don't all cats do that? I think it's sweet."

"Sweet," Jack said, disgruntled. "Last night I woke up at four in the morning to find him sprawled on my pillow in front of my face."

"Aw," Marla said. "See, he likes you."

"When I turned to face the other way—I didn't want to lie there breathing cat breath all night—you know what he did?" Jack went on. "He got up, walked around my head to the other side of the pillow, and laid down about two inches from my face again. When I backed away, he raised his head and looked at me as if I had insulted him!"

Marla laughed heartily. "Well, sure! Animals have feelings, too." She looked down at the cat, who was finishing up the last of the strip of bacon. "Was that good, Maxie?" she said in an indulgent voice.

"I thought his name was supposed to be Max," Jack said.

"Maxie's a nickname."

Jack sighed and shook his head. "I never thought you would be a pushover for a cat! Claire has a cat, but she keeps it outside."

"Claire would."

"Now, now, let's not be—catty," Jack said, amused.

"I'm not. I'm just stating a fact," Marla said. "I'm sure

Claire keeps a beautiful house. Cat fur is probably forbidden, along with bugs, crumbs and dust. No doubt her home is as perfect as a museum."

"She does keep the gallery in good order," Jack said.

"You could hire a high school kid to do that," Marla told him.

"But a high school kid couldn't do the bookkeeping."

"*I* could do the bookkeeping," she suggested.

"You already have a full-time job," he said. "More than full-time." His tone showed his discontent with the situation.

"I'm trying to cut back. The housing market is good right now, so it's been difficult," Marla said. "As for Claire, I don't see why you have to keep her on—not with the way she feels about me."

"Because she runs the gallery too well to let her go. Besides, she's polite to you whenever you come in," Jack argued.

"She may ask how I am and say everything that's proper, but I can always feel her disapproval. I know she doesn't like me. I still remember walking in that day and overhearing her trying to talk you out of marrying me."

It was a memory Marla had difficulty forgetting. She had been coming up the steps quietly to surprise Jack when she heard Claire talking in his office. "She's beneath you, Jack," Claire was saying. "She doesn't have your refinement and culture. She knows nothing about art, does she? If I were you I would think twice about marrying a woman who's so . . . well, common. She's clever and attractive, but . . ."

Claire hadn't been allowed to finish, for Jack had silenced her soundly with a few choice words. Marla was happy that Jack had spoken up for her, but the event had made Marla dislike Claire even more than she had before. She felt bad about harboring so much hostility toward someone, but she couldn't help it—especially when the woman was in such close proximity to her husband three days a week.

"She was just jealous," Jack said. "She'll get used to the idea of us being married."

Not if she still hopes she can split us up, Marla thought. It bothered her that Claire continued to bake cookies for Jack and run errands for him, as though she were his second wife, just waiting in the wings to chase his first wife offstage. Still, it didn't seem like Claire to be that premeditative. Maybe she baked cookies just because she liked to bake. Maybe she offered to run errands because she thought it was part of her job. *Maybe I'm letting my resentment get the better of me,* Marla told herself. All the same, she wished Claire would find some other man to take care of.

"I'm glad you realize she's jealous," Marla said. "She did have her eye on you."

"And she's miffed because you got me," Jack said, giving his wife a special smile. "You should be glad there's someone around as capable as Claire to run my shop. It gives me extra time—to spend with you."

Marla smiled and lowered her eyes. It was sweet of him to look at it that way. She raised her eyes to his again. A warm light flickered in their brown depths. "You always use the time well, too," she said, her voice soft.

"Don't I though." He was staring at her in that certain sexy way that always excited her. "Why don't we put some of that time to good use now?"

She smiled and then remembered she was all dressed to go to work. "Oh, darn. I'm due at the office in twenty minutes. I have an appointment . . ."

He reached across the table to grab her hand. "We'd better hurry, then."

"But Jack . . ." she said, laughing.

Gently pulling her from her chair, he picked her up in his arms. He carried her to the bedroom and set her on the bed, leaving the breakfast plates for Max to clean up.

"You'll make me late," she protested halfheartedly as she lay on the bed, letting Jack unbutton her blouse and skirt.

100

"Do you want to call your office? Is someone there?"

"Maggie's there. I'll tell her to keep my client entertained for a little while," she said, running her hand down Jack's cheek. "But we do have to hurry."

"You set the pace, darling," he said, leaning over to kiss her.

Marla could hardly talk to Maggie without giggling, for Jack was pulling off her blouse and kissing her neck and shoulders as she spoke to her co-worker. "So just give him some coffee and tell him I'll be in a little late," she said, speaking of the middle-aged man with whom she had an appointment to look at a house.

"Jack!" she said as she hung up. "How dare you," she chided him, laughing all the while. He had her bra off now and responded by gently biting her nipple. The action sent a tiny charge through Marla. "Oh . . . wait, darling," she said, growing breathless. "Let me take off everything, so we won't be delayed?"

"Fine with me."

She pulled her skirt down her hips and thighs, then her pantyhose. Jack merely watched, taking in her long, slender, bared legs, her tiny waist, and her small, perfect breasts, which bobbed lightly as she moved. She glanced at him as she tossed her panties onto the neat pile she had made on the carpeted floor. "How about you? You're still dressed." She leaned toward him and began to unbutton his shirt. "We do have to hurry." Her voice was a caress as she slid her hands beneath his opened shirt to pull it apart.

"Don't worry about that," he murmured as he stroked one soft breast, then ran his hand down her smooth skin to her waist and hip. He let her remove his shirt, then he paused to take off the rest of his clothes. As she lay back on the bed, he moved over her, bending his head to kiss her throat, then each soft, white mound as he made teasing circles around each pink nipple. "I'm ready anytime you are," he whispered.

She smiled, feeling the firm proof of his statement nudging her thigh. "Are you?" she asked innocently.

"You know damn well what you do to me," he said, his voice husky. "Just looking at you makes me feverish. Touching you sets me on fire. You make me feel so alive, Marla." He squeezed her upper arm in his strong, gentle hand, then her breast, then her hipbone, as if feeling the life and warmth in her body, wanting to experience the reality of her. "I used to be alive only when I painted. Now, with you, every day is filled with color. And when we make love, it's paradise . . ." He dug his fingers into her thick hair as he pressed her slender body into the mattress.

She closed her eyes as she felt him enter her. As she held him closer she gasped at the force of his masculinity, dominating her with wave after wave of pleasure. "Paradise," she whispered as she stroked his back. She felt his fingers tangle in her luxurious hair, holding her still for his hard, deep kisses on her eager mouth, while her body writhed beneath his. "Oh, Jack," she gasped as she broke away from his lips to breathe. "I love making love with you."

He smiled, perspiration glazing his skin. "You do, don't you! So do I, more than anything. You thrill me like nothing else ever has, like no other woman ever has." His breathing was labored, but she sensed he wanted to tell her what she meant to him. It brought tears to her eyes. His words were even more meaningful as, locked in each other's embrace, they experienced the stunning explosion, like fireworks of vivid colors piercing the quiet atmosphere of their bedroom.

Marla sighed with spent pleasure as she relaxed beneath him, still holding his body close, knowing she had given him as much happiness as she had received.

"You're wonderful," he said, nuzzling her ear as he moved to lie beside her. "You should be late for work more often."

"Work!" She sat up. "I forgot."

"Good," he said. He grabbed her hand as she got off the bed. "Someday I want to spend hours making love. I want to

102

take all the time in the world, stretch it out until we're in a frenzy so hot the sheets melt."

Marla smiled broadly at him. She liked his idea. "We're going on our honeymoon in a week. We should have lots of time then."

"I'm holding you to that," he said, then kissed her hand.

"Okay." She had to extricate her fingers gently from his grasp. "I really do have to go now."

He grinned up at her from the bed, taking in all the delightful curves of her nude body. "You might want to run a comb through your hair before you leave. Otherwise you look just fine!"

"I hope Maxie's okay," Marla said fretfully.

Jack raised his eyes to the cloudless blue sky as they waited on the sidewalk for the tour bus. In back of them was the huge, majestic Empress Hotel, where they were staying. A number of other people were also standing nearby. "Why wouldn't he be okay?" he said. "You left him big bowls of dry food and big bowls of water all over the house, plus wall-to-wall litter boxes. You'd think we were going to be away for a month, not just a week."

"He might get lonely, though," she said.

He glanced at Marla, seeing her doubtful look. "Ginger said she'd check on him, didn't she? Cats sleep most of the time anyway."

"Maxie still likes to play a lot, though," Marla said.

"I know." Jack sighed to himself as he watched a double-decker bus pull up to the curb. "When we get back, I figure the drapes will be in shreds, there'll be cat food spilled all over and everything breakable will be broken."

"Oh, one half-grown cat couldn't do all that. He's so cute."

Jack had to stifle a laugh as he listened to her coo. *"That* little monster could do it," he said. "I would have locked him in the attic."

"Now, Jack, you really ought to question your ethics when you say something like that," Marla told him. "Are you putting more value on inanimate objects than on a living creature?"

Jack had to stop and think. "The inanimate objects cost a lot to replace," he said. "But it wouldn't cost us anything to replace the cat. You got him for free. In fact, we'd have a hell of a time getting rid of him. Who'd want him?"

"Jack!"

Oh, gee, he thought. She sounded upset. He had intended only to tease her. She had gotten so attached to that pest of a cat. But this was their honeymoon, a week in beautiful old Victoria, British Columbia. They'd had to wait two weeks after the wedding because she couldn't arrange to get away from her office any sooner. Now that they were here, he wanted her to be happy, both with him and the vacation. "Yes, he's a cute cat," Jack said, putting his arm around his wife. To himself he added, *If you like white fluffy things with claws, sharp teeth and tuna-fish breath.*

"Tickets please," a good-looking young man said. He was wearing a navy blazer with the insignia of the bus line on the pocket.

Jack reached inside his jacket and gave him the two tickets they had purchased earlier in the hotel. The young man took them, giving Marla a smile as he tore off the stubs.

"Beautiful morning, isn't it? I'm Ken Davis. I'll be your tour guide today." He gave the stubs back to Jack, but never took his eyes off Marla.

She smiled back. "How long is the tour?"

"About three hours. We'll be leaving for Butchart Gardens shortly. If you have any questions, just ask," the young man told her, then passed Jack to collect tickets from the others.

"He seemed like a nice fellow," Marla said.

"Absolutely charming. A little too young for you,

though." Jack was aware a waspish tone had crept into his voice.

"Too young . . . Oh, for Pete's sake. All he did was say hello. It's part of his job."

Jack nodded and said nothing more. *She didn't need to smile at the guy so much,* he was thinking. Glancing across a large city square and busy streets, he gazed at the Parliament Buildings they had visited yesterday. He'd noticed a couple of young men looking her over then, too, as they had walked through the stately halls. Well, there wasn't much he could do about it; he'd married a gorgeous woman. It was just that he kept wondering whether she had done anything to attract their attention—made some subtle glance or movement that caught their eye and made her seem somehow available, even when she was with her husband. Maybe she wasn't aware of it. Maybe it was habit.

He shouldn't think that way, Jack told himself as he walked behind Marla, watching her shapely legs as they climbed the steps to the upper deck of the bus. She was wearing a straight skirt and a sweater today and looked slim and sexy as usual.

No, it wasn't her fault, Jack tried to assure himself. What healthy man wouldn't look at her? She had a lithe body and a graceful way of moving that naturally drew the eye. The unusual beauty of her features and her dark coloring only made you want to look more. Hadn't *he* reacted that way the first time he saw her? *The problem was, she was so quick and sure and vivacious, you had trouble knowing whether it was all for you or if she was just born that way. One flash from those bright, dark eyes and you think, She noticed me! She wants to meet me! when actually all she was doing was looking at the store window behind you,* he thought.

Jack knew. That was exactly how it was the first time he'd seen her. When he actually met her, weeks later, he mentioned having once passed her on the street, and she couldn't remember it. They ran into each other in Langley several times after that. On each occasion she gave him a stunning smile, but after the previous experience, he never felt sure she could even remember his name. It was only after she had come into his gallery and bought his seascape that he knew she had actually given him a thought or two.

Jack sat down beside his wife on the bus seat and watched her cross her long, slim legs. No, he shouldn't think Marla was a flirt. Marla was just Marla. He only wished he didn't feel like reminding her constantly that she had a husband now.

It was a thirteen-mile drive to Butchart Gardens, with splendid views of lakes and sloping farmland along the way. In his mind's eye Jack saw dozens of paintings he would like to do of the peaceful landscape. When they arrived, the tour guide led them slowly through the thirty-five-acre garden, which had once been an abandoned limestone quarry.

"It all started in 1904, when Jennie Butchart decided to transform the quarry into a sunken garden," Ken Davis told the group. He explained that Jennie Butchart was the wife of Robert Pim Butchart, who had had a very successful cement company. The old quarry was part of their 130-acre estate. Over the years Mrs. Butchart had personally collected many plants from all over the world to beautify it.

Eventually the guide led the group to a switchback staircase that took them to the floor of the quarry. Pointing, he said, "There you can see Rock Island. There's an observation spot on top. It towers over the large artificial lake you see below, which fills what was once a particularly deep pocket of limestone. On the left is a waterfall. It flows from the top of the quarry, splashes down to a pool, then forms a small stream that meanders to the lake."

Jack was impressed with the beauty and color and variety of plants about them, all flawlessly kept. Later, when Marla said to him, "This is lovely, isn't it?" as they were approaching the lake, he was more than ready to agree.

But Jack never had a chance to answer. Ken Davis, who

always seemed to be nearby, said, "Yes, this is my favorite spot in the park."

Who gives a damn, Jack thought. There were about twenty people in their group. He wished their eager tour guide would give more attention to some of the others.

"What are those plants that border the lake?" Marla asked, her brown eyes full of interest as she glanced at the dark-haired young man.

"Those are azaleas," Davis said. "The rest is flowering cherry, plum, and dwarf Japanese maple. The Japanese maple is represented by both the cut-leaf and the regular varieties."

"How do you remember all that?" she said with a smile.

Davis grinned. "It's not hard," he said.

He had all the cocky confidence of a twenty-two-year-old, which was about the age Jack guessed him to be. Jack remembered that he had been equally obnoxious when he was that age. Only he didn't go around trying to make an impression on married women. Why was Marla humoring the little beggar?

"A botanist, are you?" Jack asked.

"I'm doing graduate work in that field, yes," Davis said, straightening his necktie in a preening manner.

"How come you aren't at school, then?" Jack asked.

Marla gave Jack a sharp, questioning look.

"I only attend classes two days a week. I work the rest of the time," Davis said.

"Putting yourself through school?" Marla asked.

"Yes."

"With all the studying you must have to do, I imagine it's difficult to work, too," Marla said, her tone sympathetic.

"Oh, it's not so bad," the young man responded. "I learn a lot working here, and I enjoy the job—especially some of the people I meet." He was turned toward Marla, so Jack had only a partial view of Davis's face, but Jack was sure the smile he was giving her was far too intimate.

"Shouldn't we be moving on?" Jack said, his voice testy.

As Davis directed the group onward, Marla said quietly to Jack, "What's wrong? Why are you so annoyed?"

Jack looked around and waited until the others moved ahead before answering. "I don't like the way he's hanging all over you."

Marla seemed mystified. "No, he isn't. He just answered the question I asked."

"It seems like he's been at your elbow to answer your questions ever since we got here," Jack said, beginning to fume. He knew his jealousy was showing. *So what?* he told himself. He had every right to keep his wife away from other men, didn't he? Especially if his wife was a first-class flirt. "And why do you have so many questions? I thought you were about as interested in plants as you are in cooking!"

"Well, being here in this place makes me interested in plants. I've never learned much about them," she said. "I don't know why that should bother you."

"If our guide was female, would you be so interested?" Jack said in a cutting tone.

Marla stared at him, her dark eyes growing steely. "I see. Married two weeks and we're back to that already. I can't even talk to another man without you making something out of it!"

Jack didn't know what to think. She seemed confident of her guiltless behavior. But then she always did. He remembered that night months ago, when he and Ginger had found her at Devin's home. She had been very sure of herself and her innocence then, too, even though she had already admitted to Ginger that she was attracted to Devin.

"We'd better catch up with the group or he'll miss you," Jack muttered. He began walking on up the path, leaving Marla to follow. For a second he was afraid she wouldn't, but in a moment she was at his side, in step with him.

By the time they reached the Japanese Garden, Jack was having guilty feelings about what he had said to Marla. She hadn't spoken a word to him for the last half-hour. The freeze-out was getting to him. Neither had she said anything much to the tour guide. Jack began to realize he had been rather ridiculous, thinking that Marla might be flirting with Ken Davis. After all, she had been with Jack every minute, and all she had done was ask a few questions. She couldn't help it if the young guy admired her. Now it seemed Jack had spoiled her day—and his own, too.

"Careful, don't trip," he said, taking his wife's arm. She looked surprised. Jack could understand her reaction. The walk was smoothly paved and she was in no danger of tripping on anything. It was just an excuse to break the ice. "Are those shoes comfortable? You aren't getting tired, are you?"

"No, these are good walking shoes," she said coolly.

At least she was speaking to him again, Jack thought. The guide was edging toward them once more. Jack stifled a sigh and vowed to say nothing unpleasant no matter what. They were walking along a path that followed winding pools shaded by weeping willows. Davis pointed out a certain plant to Marla and said, "This is the blue poppy of Tibet. It's very rare. Mrs. Butchart was one of the first to import it to North America."

"How nice," was all Marla said.

Jack felt even more guilty now, listening to his wife curb her natural friendliness.

"Is it actually from Tibet?" Jack asked with feigned interest. Davis went into a long discourse on the poppy, to which Jack only half listened. He had asked the question because he wanted things back on an even keel for Marla's sake. *Let the poor guy nose around her,* Jack had decided. *I'm the one she'll be going back to the hotel with,* he reminded himself, feeling a little smug now.

But he lost some of the smugness when he and Marla stopped for a light lunch at the coffee bar. There was an allotment of time for refreshments before the bus returned to the hotel. Marla was still distant and cool, and Jack wasn't sure how to make things right with her. He supposed being straightforward was the best way to handle it. But it was also the most painful, since it required him to admit he was wrong.

"How's the salad?"

"Fine," she said, poking her fork into a piece of cheese.

"Look, I'm sorry I gave you a hard time," he said. "I'm just . . . hopelessly jealous of any man who comes near my gorgeous wife." Flattery ought to help, Jack thought.

She looked at him, her dark eyes steady. "Go on," she said.

Jack cleared his throat. "I . . . it was just a gut reaction on my part. I guess I haven't managed to bury the past completely yet. I'll . . . work on it," he said, lowering his eyes.

"When we agreed to marry, I promised you you could trust me, Jack. I haven't broken that promise, and I won't. I wish you would believe that."

"I do," he said quietly, looking at her again.

Her eyes warmed, and she smiled. It was like a rainbow after a shower. Jack relaxed. *She is wonderful, isn't she,* Jack said to himself as he watched her go back to eating her salad. Tough and sweet and beautiful. And he was the lucky man who had her!

"You're certainly looking pleased with yourself," she said, after swallowing a mouthful. Her eyes sparkled as she looked at him now. It turned him on.

"I'm thinking about the bus ride back," he said, picking up his sandwich.

"What about it?"

"I think we should take the very back seat on the upper deck."

"Why?"

"So we can neck."

She laughed. "Like teenagers?"

"Yes. Only we won't have to worry about what our parents would think if they found out," he said, eyes dancing with amusement.

"And we have that beautiful hotel room to finish things off in," Marla said, her voice a little sultry now.

Jack smiled at her knowingly. What a sexy woman.

"Did you enjoy the tour?" Ken Davis's voice startled him.

Oh, get lost, Jack thought. The young man was looking at Marla, but Jack answered. "Great! Will the bus be leaving soon?"

"Ten minutes," Davis said.

"We'll be there," Jack told him. "I saw some of the others go into the gift shop. You'd better check up on them."

"I . . . well . . . see you at the bus," Davis said, looking a little off-balance.

Marla smiled as he walked away. "He did turn out to be kind of a pest, didn't he?" she said quietly.

"I'm glad to hear you agree with me!" Jack said, feeling triumphant.

"A woman must always agree with her husband," Marla said, demure and kittenish.

Now she was needling him, Jack thought, taking in her provocative gaze. Like her cat, she loved to play. He shook his finger at her. "Wait till I get you on the backseat of the bus, woman. We'll just see who's boss!"

"I can't wait," she said.

Jack couldn't either. Her voice sounded just like a purr, and he was impatient to stroke and pet her.

"Jack!" Marla protested with a giggle, pushing Jack's probing hand out of the V neckline of her royal blue sweater. "What if someone saw us?" she whispered.

Jack glanced forward at the seven or eight people on the upper deck of the bus. The tour guide was down on the lower level with the bus driver. "They're all half asleep up ahead," Jack said, seeking out her soft breasts again. "Why should they care anyway?"

She let him have his way, though she felt a little embarrassed. Her skirt was already pushed halfway up her thighs by his eager hands. But she decided she liked being manhandled by her husband on the backseat of a bus. Maybe it meant she didn't have any class—she was sure it was something Claire would never do. But who cared? Certainly not Jack!

She closed her eyes and sank against him as he kissed her again. It was surprising that they should be so close now. She had been hurt and upset with him earlier, when he had practically accused her of flirting with the tour guide, of all people. And now, a while later, it was all forgotten. The many facets of a love relationship between a man and a woman could certainly be confusing. But as long as things ended this way, she could live with it.

She made a small sound of pleasure. Jack's fingers had slipped into her sweater neckline and under her bra, finding her nipple. He was teasing it in that special way of his, and it was driving her to delightful madness. "Jack," she chided, giving him little kisses on his neck and chin, "you'll get me too aroused."

"Why should I be the only one to suffer?" He looked down at her with eyes like embers.

She slipped her hand below and realized he had his problems, too. Grinning at him, she said, "Well, it's your own fault, you know. This backseat idea was all yours."

"You agreed to it, didn't you? Who was it who said she couldn't wait?"

"I know," she admitted, running her hand up and down his shirt beneath his jacket. "Now I can't wait to get to our hotel room."

"Me either." He took her in his arms and kissed her again. This time his roving hand returned to her smooth thighs beneath her skirt, moving slowly up her pantyhose to her rounded hip.

They were so engrossed, they barely heard Ken Davis's voice over the speaker saying they had arrived at the hotel and thanking everyone for taking the tour.

Breathless, their clothes a little disheveled, Marla and Jack were the last ones off the bus.

"Hope—you enjoyed the trip," Ken said, taking in the flush of sensuality in Marla's eyes and her mussed hair as she stepped off the bus. He seemed a little shocked.

"We did!" Jack said and hurried Marla on toward the hotel.

"I wonder what he must have thought," Marla said. She was a little discomfited by the tour guide's reaction.

"Don't worry," Jack said with a smile. "He's too young to know about wanton women like you."

"Jack!"

"*I'm* not, though." He lifted one brow archly as he looked down at her.

"I see!" she said, a little miffed. "Well, let's at least try to walk through the hotel lobby with a little dignity." She broke away from his arm, which was tightly about her waist, pressing her against him. After shifting her sweater back into place, she tugged up on the neckline that had gotten rather stretched. She straightened her skirt then and tried to smooth her hair with her fingertips.

Jack was watching her. "That's good enough. I'll just muss you all up again when we get to the room."

She tried to give him a stern look, but wound up stifling a laugh. How could a man be so adorable and infuriating?

Smiling, he put out his elbow. "If you'll take my arm, Mrs. Whiting, I will escort you through the lobby."

She sighed in exasperation and took his arm. Their walk through the elegant huge lobby of the old hotel was decorous enough. But when they reached the long empty hall at the end of which their room was located, Jack began to get out of hand again.

He put his arm at her waist and caught her up against him again, so that his thigh brushed hers as they walked. He tugged at her sweater, pulling the neckline down almost to the top of her bra, and gazed with hungering eyes at her revealed cleavage. Pausing for a moment, he bent to kiss the soft flesh.

"Jack," she protested, but he stopped her by kissing her on the mouth. "Someone could come down the hall any minute!" she said when she had managed to pull away a bit.

"Let them. We haven't gotten to the X-rated stage yet," he told her with an intimate smile.

"Oh, Jack!" she reproved him, but she couldn't keep from laughing.

At last they reached their door, and soon they were in their room. Sunlight was pouring in through the sheer drapes on the windows. Everything was quiet and bright in the beautifully decorated room with its amber carpet and coordinated bedspread. The maid had been in to clean, and everything was in perfect order.

Jack was staring at Marla as she stood near the dresser, where she had set her purse. His blue eyes were luminous with reflected sunlight from the high windows. "You look wonderful backlighted like that," he said, coming close to her. "I should paint you like this."

"Really?" Marla said. She was eager for him to paint her again. The portrait he had done would go to her mother in a few months, and she hated the thought of parting with it. "How should I dress for this one?"

"How about not dressing at all?"

"Jack, a nude painting—of me? Where would we hang it?"

"In our bedroom."

She chuckled. "That would be fine for you. Would you do a matching self-portrait for me?"

He laughed. "What a bore! *You'll* have to take lessons in oil painting if you want one of me. Meanwhile, how about taking those clothes off, so I can get some ideas."

"I think you have ideas already."

"I mean for poses," he said, putting his hands at her waist and pulling her against him.

"I bet! You're not thinking about art right now," she teased.

"You want to bet? All right, let's get these off!" He began pushing her sweater up over her breasts and arms. Throwing the sweater aside, he unbuttoned her skirt and let it fall to the floor, then her bra. "You do the rest," he said, his tone masterful and impatient. He took off his jacket and shirt while she obediently removed her shoes, pantyhose and panties. She stood in front of him then, hands on her hips, poking out her chest at him in a mocking, provocative way.

"Well, how would you like me to pose?" Her voice was sweet and sultry.

He looked her over a moment. "How about on the bed?"

"I thought so," she said with a knowing grin. "You lose the bet!"

He was unbuckling his belt now. "Okay, so I lose. I'm not proud."

"I'm not either," she said, laughing, and helped him by unzipping his pants. In moments he was undressed, too. "Make love to me?" she said, slipping her arms around his neck.

"You bet," he whispered and picked her up in his arms. He brought her to the bed and lay down alongside her.

As she enjoyed the feel of his gentle hand over her stomach and abdomen, she said, "Remember you told me you wanted to spend hours making love, prolong it until we can't hold ourselves back any longer?"

He nodded. "I don't think I can quite manage that at the moment. But I'm willing to spend the rest of the afternoon in this bed with you, testing our stamina." He gave her a little grin.

She smiled back. "Okay. I don't think I can hold out right now, either. Not after all your work on the bus. I . . ." She closed her eyes at the sudden pleasure of his hands softly moving over her bare breasts. "Oh, Jack . . . I love the way you touch me."

"I love to touch you," he said. "And kiss you." He kissed her mouth. "And bite you." He bit her shoulder, and the sensation made her squirm and giggle. "And lick you." His lips and tongue found one rosy nipple, sending delicate shock waves through her. His mouth moved to her other nipple then, while his hand slid down to the tender secret place between her thighs. She was already moist with desire, and his light touch went to the quick of her. She gasped sharply at the electrifying sensation.

"Oh, Jack," she said weakly, "no more now. Please . . . come to me."

As he moved over her, she moaned in overwhelming pleasure at the thrust of his masculinity deep within her. His body settled warmly over hers, pressing her into the bed covers. She put her arms around him to hold him tightly as they moved in unison. The feel of him in her embrace made her smile, reveling in the glorious experience of being loved and wanted, of giving and receiving.

The rhythm of their movements grew faster and stronger, out of control, until it became a burning, erotic friction that soon erupted like lava from a volcano. Heat poured over Marla and she felt that marvelous sensation of falling freely as her body trembled in ecstasy. Her heartbeat was light and fast beneath Jack as she clung to him, and she could feel the heavy pounding of his heart as he came to his own fulfillment. She smiled in contentment as, gradually, he relaxed over her and she softly stroked his back.

They dozed languidly for a while. When they awoke, in their cozy comfortable haze, she and Jack set about the pleasurable business of discovering how long they could make their lovemaking last. Hours later, after resting from the monumentally successful endurance test, Marla wasn't surprised when Jack wanted to see if they could repeat or better their record. She kept up with him, returning each languorous stroke, each deep, searching kiss, each gently teasing caress, each softly murmured endearment. Toward evening, as the shadows deepened in the room, the tension in her body just below her stomach had again mounted to a point that was no longer bearable, though she would have wished to prolong it even more if she could, she loved his lovemaking so.

"Oh, Jack . . . I can't hold back . . ." she murmured to him in defeat.

"I can't either," he said in a labored whisper, even as she felt her body break free to a wondrous, ecstatic climax that left her blissfully exhausted in Jack's arms.

When they went down to the hotel dining room for a late dinner, Marla was tired but very happy. She hadn't known before the extent of her own capacity for sensual pleasure, or Jack's, either. He was a veritable powerhouse.

They were curiously quiet for a while after the waiter had taken their order, content just to be together, absorbing the elegant surroundings. When the waiter had poured their wine, however, Jack lifted his crystal glass in a toast.

"To my wife," he said with a soft smile, though his voice and eyes conveyed deeply felt emotion. "With you, real life is better than any fantasy I could imagine. I love you, Marla."

His unexpected, sincere words swept over Marla like a wave. Tears filled her eyes. With a smile that quivered, she raised her glass. She wanted to respond with words as beautiful as his, but all her voice would allow was a hushed, "I love you, too."

CHAPTER SEVEN

"I'm hoping to get home early today, for a change," Marla said to Maggie Sommers, her favorite co-worker at the real estate office on Second Street. It was about six weeks after she and Jack had returned from their relaxing, intimate honeymoon. Marla had been working so hard lately, she felt like she could use another vacation already.

"I'd like to go home early, too," Maggie said. She was a motherly-looking lady of about fifty-five. Plump, with salt-and-pepper short hair, she had been working at the office even longer than Marla had. "It used to be weekdays weren't so bad as the weekends, but lately—gee, I can't tell one day from another anymore. It's nice to have business jumping, but I almost wish interest rates would go up again so we could take a breather."

"Yes," Marla agreed. "Jack hasn't been too happy about it. I had been planning to quit or at least cut back, but it's hard to. I'd hate to dump my workload on you and the others. And then when I think of all the money I can make now, while the market is so good, I tell myself this would be a stupid time to quit."

Maggie chuckled. "I know what you mean. But you're right; we shouldn't complain. My sales last month were the best ever since I got into real estate. I don't care how tired I am, I'm hanging in there!"

Marla smiled, but couldn't quite bring herself to agree. She would gladly quit if the circumstances were right. The main problem was, she still hadn't figured out what she would do instead of real estate. She didn't want to stay home, and she didn't have any interest in motherhood, at least not yet. What would she do if she quit? She had thought she'd buy some small business and run it, but what business? It would have to be close to home to suit her and Jack, and there wasn't a great deal of choice in Langley or any of the other small towns on the island. There was already an overabundance of antique stores in the area. Operating a restaurant would be too closely aligned to cooking to appeal to her. She had even thought of running a movie theater, but the owner of the one in Langley had no interest in selling. Lately she had been thinking about opening a clothing store, since she did have some interest in stylish women's apparel, but her real estate business was so brisk, she hadn't had any time to investigate the possibilities.

Marla was finishing up some paperwork about fifteen minutes later. Glancing at her watch, she saw it was five-thirty. Maybe she would get home at a decent time this evening after all.

She had not even finished the thought when a young man walked into the office. Marla, Maggie, the secretary, and two other agents were in at the moment. The man glanced over the open office, then went straight to Marla's desk.

"Excuse me," he said. "I'm thinking of buying a home on the island. I was hoping someone could show me what was available."

He was about thirty, Marla guessed—the proverbial dark handsome man. His hair was black, his eyebrows thick, his nose slightly crooked, his mouth full and sensuously curved. He appeared broad-shouldered and muscular beneath his jacket and open-collared shirt. A gold chain was around his thick neck. He was thoroughly masculine, but Marla sensed something in his looks and manner she didn't like. It didn't matter, however. She was bent on going home as soon as possible.

"We have many properties available," she told him with a smile. She turned in her swivel chair toward Maggie, whose desk was in back of hers. "This is Maggie Sommers. I'm sure she'll be very helpful."

Maggie looked a little surprised, but she quickly said hello to the potential buyer.

The man nodded at Maggie and cleared his throat. "I'm sure she would be," he said, looking at Marla again. "But I think you would have a better feel for the type of place I'm looking for."

"Maggie has more experience in real estate than I do," Marla said, determined not to take on extra work she didn't want.

"I'm sure she does, and if you weren't here, I'd be happy to put myself under her care," he said smoothly. "But I asked you first. You are a real estate agent, aren't you?" he said to Marla. His eyes were brown, but much darker than Marla's, so dark they were almost black. She felt she couldn't read what was in their depths, and it made her a little uneasy.

"Yes, I'm an agent. I was just about to go home," she said, deciding honesty might be the best policy.

"Oh. Well," he said in an amiable tone, "how about tomorrow morning then? Anytime you want, actually. I'm on vacation for two weeks, so my schedule is open."

"Did someone recommend me to you?" she asked, curious.

"A friend recommended this realty company," he said. "When I came in I saw you and decided you were the right agent for me."

"Why?"

He shrugged. "Good vibrations, I guess."

Marla made a dubious half-smile and glanced at Maggie.

"I guess we can't argue with vibrations," Maggie said good-naturedly.

120

"I'm glad you're so understanding," the man said to Maggie.

There was an oily politeness about him Marla didn't like. It seemed like learned behavior calculated to please, not a trait that came naturally. Unfortunately, she had little choice now but to take him on as a client.

"All right," she said, stifling a sigh. "Tomorrow at ten?"

"Great," he said. "And what's your name?"

"Marla Whiting."

"Marla," he repeated with a smile. "Interesting."

"What's yours?" Marla picked up her pen to write it on her calendar.

"Rory Preston."

She wrote the name down. "Okay," she said, keeping her tone light. "Tomorrow morning it is."

He smiled cordially. "See you then," he said and walked out.

"Rory?" Marla said to Maggie when he was gone. *"Rory?"* It amused Marla. She didn't know him, but the name seemed to fit.

"I think there used to be an actor named Rory," Maggie said.

"I bet this guy's an actor, too," Marla told her. "Not for the stage or screen, though."

"One who puts on a good act for women?" Maggie said, chuckling.

"That's exactly what I was thinking." Marla was glad that Maggie seemed to have the same perceptions about the man. "He reminds me of those cars you see with the make written in big letters across the top of the windshield—you know, Porsche or Rabbit? He ought to have *Stud* stamped across his forehead!"

Maggie laughed. "He sure was set on you. Ah, if I were only twenty-five years younger," she said dreamily.

"Don't envy me!" Marla said. "I'm sure not looking forward to showing him around."

She forgot about Rory Preston by the time she got home that evening. Jack was glad to see her home early and let her know it with a bear hug and a kiss.

"How about if I take you out to dinner?" he asked.

"I'd love it!"

They drove up to Oak Harbor, the largest town on the island, to a new seafood restaurant Jack said he'd heard about. Both ordered fresh salmon. As they sipped white wine, waiting for their dinner, Marla said, "Ginger called me at work today. She just found out from the doctor that she's going to have a baby."

"Well, good for her!" Jack replied. "She wanted one, didn't she?"

"Yes, she's very happy. And Devin is thrilled, she said."

Jack nodded. "I'm glad." His tone showed genuine good-will, and Marla was relieved. Now that Devin was going to be a family man, maybe Jack would be able to stop regarding him as the man Marla had once been interested in. She didn't think Jack had ever blamed Devin, and there was no reason the two men couldn't be friends. Marla and Jack had been at Devin and Ginger's wedding, and that uneasy day was the last time the four had been together. She hoped that soon they could all go out again, this time as friends.

"Is she going to sell her shop, then?" Jack asked.

Marla's smile was wistful. "Yes. She asked if I wanted to buy it. I told her I'd like to, but I didn't think I'd ever know enough about cooking to sell anything."

Jack chuckled. "I think that was wise. Things settling down at work yet?"

"No. Someone came in just before I left, wanting me to show him some homes. I told him to come back tomorrow."

"Good," Jack said. "It shows you can make your own hours if you want to."

"Yes, but at the risk of losing some good profits."

"This guy didn't mind waiting, did he?" Jack said.

"No, I guess not." Marla let the subject go at that. She

didn't feel like talking about Rory Preston. No use worrying her jealousy-prone husband about a man she was sure she could handle. "Who told you about this restaurant?" she asked, changing the subject. "It has a nice, quiet atmosphere."

"Claire heard about it," Jack said.

"Oh," Marla replied with a sigh.

Jack chuckled. "Now, now. Don't tell me you're still harboring a grudge against her. She said she ran into you on Second Street on her lunch hour the other day, and that you two had a nice little chat. She seems to have put aside her animosity toward you."

Marla glanced over the sparkling silverware on the white tablecloth in front of her. It figured that Claire would have given him the impression that everything was fine between the two of them. If only for the fact that Jack was her employer, Claire would want him to think she got along with his wife. Marla supposed one could describe the brief conversation she had had with Claire on Second Street as a "nice little chat." It had been that—on the surface.

Marla had just parked her car and was walking toward her office when she saw Claire coming out of the drugstore down the street. As soon as they eyed each other, Claire quickly looked away. Then, apparently deciding she'd better be cordial, she walked up to Marla with a fixed smile on her face.

"Well, hello!" she had said. Marla heard the forced friendliness in her voice. "How are you? I'm surprised I haven't seen you more often around town."

"Fate just hasn't thrown us together, I guess." Marla's tone was less eager, but she tried to be amiable. "How are things at the studio?"

"We sold one of Jack's paintings this morning. You know, the seascape with all the birds? I'm just about to stop in at the café to pick up some lunch for him."

The information made Marla's throat tighten. "You

shouldn't spoil him like that," she said sweetly. "Let him get his own lunch. He needs the exercise."

"Oh, I don't mind. He works so hard. I have to get something for myself anyway." There was a hardness in Claire's eyes then that Marla had never seen in the woman before. It was as though she was going to cling to whatever part of Jack she could have, and she would not let even his wife interfere. Marla also sensed that Claire was perceiving Marla's uneasiness, and that the woman felt some triumph in that.

They had parted then on the same note of false friendship as they had begun. And then, apparently, Claire had gone back to the gallery and told Jack she had just had a nice little chat with Marla, knowing it was something Jack would want to hear. It also meant that if Marla continued to show resentment concerning Claire, it would look like it was one-sided, as though Claire was willing to be friends but Marla wasn't. Claire, Marla was learning, was more clever than she had thought.

"Yes, we're good buddies now," Marla said to Jack, a waspishness in her wit. "Claire and I are just like two moths in a mitten—and you own the mitten."

Jack smiled at her curiously. "What's that supposed to mean?"

Marla smiled and shrugged. "I don't know. Whichever of us moths chews the fastest gets the hand, I suppose."

"Maybe someday you'll interpret that for me," Jack said as the waiter put a plate of salmon in front of Marla.

Marla's expression was enigmatic as the waiter set a similar plate in front of Jack. Jack wasn't quite so thick as he was pretending, she suspected. She sensed he rather enjoyed Marla's jealousy over him. Maybe he also enjoyed Claire's waiting on him hand and foot; it was something he didn't get at home. In any case, he showed no signs of wanting to let Claire go, and Marla knew better than to make any more fuss about it.

But Claire's continued presence in their lives was perhaps the main reason Marla wanted a job with better hours. Working late and leaving Jack alone evenings so often might make him more prone to enjoy Claire's company on the days she was at the gallery. Marla didn't even have the luxury of meeting him for lunch, because her schedule was unpredictable and she was often tied up with clients. But there was Claire, working in close proximity to him three days a week, bringing him cookies, running errands for him, always amiable, always immaculate and pretty, always ready to discuss art—at least that was what Jack said they talked about. Claire was a quiet, insidious force to be reckoned with. If Marla continued to neglect her husband because of her job, she feared Jack might find other things about Claire to interest him besides her conversational abilities and her bookkeeping skills.

After Marla and Jack ended the evening by making love, however, she decided not to worry about Claire. As she cuddled sleepily against him beneath the covers, the sublime intimacy she had just shared with Jack made her feel secure that no one else could ever come between them.

Rory Preston showed up at Marla's office promptly at ten the next morning.

"Hello, Marla," he said, as if they were old friends. She was alone in the office at the moment, except for the secretary.

"Hello," she said, stifling the urge to say, *I'm Mrs. Whiting to you.* "So—what sort of home are you looking for and how much are you willing to spend?" She motioned to him to take the seat at her desk.

He sat down and leaned toward her, both elbows on the desktop. Today he was wearing a brown leather jacket over a sport shirt. The thick gold chain gleamed at his neck. Marla instinctively felt like backing away, but didn't. "Something modern. Something near a beach, and price is really no object," he said.

"Okay. How big? How many bedrooms?"

"One's enough," he said. A glimmer played over his dark eyes.

Marla glanced away. "Is this to be a vacation home or a permanent home?"

"I live in Seattle. I wanted a getaway sort of place. You know, somewhere to relax on my days off. A place to bring a friend."

Female, no doubt, Marla thought as she picked up the current multiple listing book. "You're single, then? No family to accommodate?"

"Wouldn't have it any other way," he said smugly.

She smiled a little. "I see. What business are you in?" she asked as she continued to leaf through the listing book.

"I'm a salesman for an import auto dealership in Seattle." He named some very expensive foreign cars he sold.

How appropriate, Marla thought, remembering how she had joked with Maggie. She turned the book toward him, opened at a particular page. "You might glance over these listings to see if any sound suitable."

He gave the page a perfunctory glance, then leaned back. "I'd rather see the homes themselves."

"All of them?"

"Yes. I can't get a feel for a place by looking at these little write-ups and photos. I have to see them to figure out what I want."

"That would take a lot of time. Don't you think you could narrow it down . . ."

"No, I want to see everything available, just like I'd want to see every car available before I bought one. We don't have to do it all in one day. I told you yesterday, I'm on vacation. We can spend the next two weeks looking at homes." He grinned, flashing his white teeth at her then, as if the prospect sounded like fun.

"I do have other buyers," Marla said. There was no way she was going to see him every day for two weeks.

"Squeeze me in where you can. I'm patient."

After making several phone calls to the owners of some of the homes that were for sale, Marla resignedly led him outside to her car. She took him to five houses over the next three hours, located on various parts of the small island. He took his time looking over each, though as she talked to him, she found he didn't seem to have a clear idea of what he wanted. He liked a small one-bedroom home she had shown him as much as a four-bedroom house she had also shown him because it was close by. This made him interested in seeing many other homes in her listing book that she at first had thought she could rule out because of size.

Finally, at about one-thirty, she said, "Well, I want to take my lunch break now, and then I have to get back to the office. Maybe we could look some more another day." They had just finished viewing a home near Oak Harbor.

"Sure. How about having lunch together?"

"Oh, no . . . I'm meeting my husband," she told him as they walked to her car.

"I was afraid of that." He grinned slightly as he looked her over.

"Of what?"

"That you'd be married."

She raised her left hand and flashed her wide gold wedding band with its large diamond at the center. "I don't wear this ring for nothing." She knew he must have noticed it already.

To her surprise, he grabbed her hand. "That's some ring! No wonder you married him."

Impatiently Marla extracted her hand from his grasp. She resented his familiarity and his insinuation that she had married just to get a big diamond. "I married for many reasons," she said. *None of which this guy would understand,* she thought.

"Love?" he said. His tone was a little snide. He looked at her, amusement in his black-brown eyes.

"Yes."

"You must be pretty good to rate a diamond that size," he said, gazing down at her long legs, then up to her breasts. She was wearing a skirted brown suit, and she quickly buttoned the jacket over her blouse. Her eyes became bright with anger.

"You don't have to take that like an insult. I meant it as a compliment. You're a beautiful woman." His eyes were taking on a certain sheen she didn't like.

She got into her car and started the motor, fuming at the man's audacity. He hurried around to the other side to get in.

"Hey, don't drive away without me!" he said, laughing. "I'm lost here."

Marla said nothing but kept her eyes directed at the windshield as she drove away from the curb into the street.

After several minutes of icy silence in the car, Preston said, "Look, I'm sorry. Don't be so touchy. Why don't you let me buy you lunch to make up for it?"

"I told you," she said in a calm, cold voice, "I'm having lunch with my husband." It wasn't true, but she'd go to the gallery and make it true if she had to.

"Okay, okay," Preston said. "He's a lucky guy." After several more minutes of silence as Marla headed onto the road to take them back to Langley, Preston asked, "How'd you meet your husband?"

Marla didn't feel like talking to the man at all, but he was a buyer, and he had apologized. "In town."

"Through your work? Was he selling some property?"

"No."

"I'm surprised. I thought your job would be a great way to meet men," he said.

Marla sighed. "That isn't why I work in real estate."

"But you do meet a lot of men?"

She hesitated. "I suppose so."

"Ever had a fling with any of them?" he asked.

Marla turned and stared at him. She couldn't believe the question. "No!"

He laughed. "Why are you so shocked? One of the advantages of being a salesman is the people I meet. Some pretty foxy ladies come in to buy my cars. You look like a foxy lady —I should think you'd take advantage of your situation. You must meet some rich men looking for expensive homes."

"Your philosophy of life is somewhat different from mine," she said, keeping to herself the cutting reply she would have liked to give him.

"You're married, so you don't play around, is that it?" he said.

"Yes."

He nodded. "All right. I respect that. How long have you been married?"

"Two months."

He chuckled again. She didn't see why he found everything so funny. "That's all? So not long ago you were still a swinging single."

"Not exactly," she said, gritting her teeth. She was driving as fast as she dared to get back to Langley so she could rid herself of Rory Preston.

"Oh, come on! You weren't any wallflower, I can tell that."

He was smiling at her again as he eyed her. She could see him from the corner of her eye. "I dated my husband for quite a while before I married him," she said.

"Heavy relationship?"

Marla pressed her lips together and didn't answer.

He smiled knowingly at her silence. "Like I said, he must have thought you were dynamite to give you a rock like that. I bet you are, too."

Marla gripped the steering wheel tightly. Finally they

129

were coming into Langley. "Look, Mr. Preston," she said in clipped, cutting tones. "I don't care for your conversation. My personal life is none of your business. Maybe you'd better find yourself another agent."

"Now wait," he said as she pulled up in front of her office. "I didn't mean anything . . ." She got out of the car and slammed the door. Quickly he got out and followed her. He caught her arm just outside her office door. "Marla, I'm sorry. Really. Don't pay any attention to what I said. Salesmen like to talk, you know that. I didn't mean to insult you, and I'm sincerely sorry if I have."

Suddenly he was all politeness, as he had been the day before when he first walked into the office. "All right, I accept your apology," Marla said, barely keeping her patience. "But I would prefer not to show you any more homes."

"You mean you'd give up a good commission? I'm pretty well heeled. I can afford to buy what I want. Your percentage wouldn't be bad," he said.

His clothes were expensive-looking, and Marla suspected that what he said about his financial status was probably true. But that didn't matter. She wanted to tell him he wasn't worth any price. "I'm not looking to get rich," she said.

He smiled. "You're a tough lady! You know how to take care of yourself around men—you did just fine today. Just because I like to admire a beautiful woman, why let that bother you?"

"There are plenty of other real estate agents—"

"But I want the best," he persisted. "I'm a salesman. I can recognize another good salesperson when I see one. You know your turf, I can tell, and that's what I want. And from your point of view, it's not smart to dump a good potential buyer. I'm surprised you'd even think of doing that."

Marla raised her eyes to the sky. Getting rid of him was no easy task.

"I'm really, honestly sorry." His voice was extraordinarily

130

contrite now. "I'll mind my manners, I promise. I just want a good house, and I need you to help me find it."

She slowly exhaled a long sigh. Of course, she didn't believe him. But, yes, she could take care of herself, and it would be unprofessional of her to drop him because he had made a few suggestive remarks. Women in all types of business had to expect that from time to time. "All right."

"Tomorrow?" he said, smiling again.

"Yes." She turned away without another glance and walked into her office.

The next morning Preston showed up at about nine-thirty, and Marla showed him more homes. To her relief, around noontime he found one he seemed to like quite a bit. It was a house already vacated by its owner, located in the North Bluff area past Holmes Harbor.

"This looks just about perfect," he said, walking around the large, empty living room with its almost-new plush carpeting, its huge fireplace and built-in wet bar. The master bedroom was also spacious, with its own fireplace, and he particularly seemed to like that. Marla could guess why. He took a perfunctory look at the kitchen, dining room and extra bedroom.

"Would you like to make an offer?" she asked.

"For the house?" he said with a little grin.

"Yes." She kept her patience; she was getting used to his banter. Words were harmless, she kept telling herself.

He was thoughtful for a moment. "I'd better think it over —you know, sleep on it?" He smiled at her again. "Yes, I'll think it over, check my finances and let you know. I may want to look at it again."

"Of course," Marla said. *Good,* she thought. *This may be more painless than I anticipated.*

Feeling more relaxed now, she drove him back to Langley at about one o'clock. He talked about the house, whether she thought the owner would come down in price and by how much. It was a conversation she was comfortable with. She

131

turned onto Second Street in Langley and pulled up in front of her office.

"Should I expect to hear from you about the house tomorrow?" she asked before getting out of the car.

"You should," he said. He edged toward her a bit. "You've been very helpful today. Like I said, I picked the right saleslady. And you," he said, moving even closer now, so that she backed away slightly, "are some lady!"

All at once, before she could believe it, he had closed the space left between them, put his arms around her and kissed her forcefully on the mouth. She felt his wet lips and then his tongue trying to gain entry. Immediate revulsion welled up inside her and she pushed hard against him to break away. "Stop it!" she hissed, reaching up to slap him.

"Hey!" he said, chuckling as he ducked her hand. "I knew you'd be a little wildcat! See you tomorrow, honey."

"Don't you dare come—" Before she could finish, he had gotten out of the car and was walking jauntily up the sidewalk. Marla was trembling with rage, but she knew better than to run after him on the street and vent her anger. It wasn't wise to make a scene in such a small town. It was just a kiss, however disgusting, she told herself as she got out of her car. So he had to have his fun. She should have expected it. Next time she'd be better prepared. And once he'd bought his damned house, he'd be out of her hair.

As she walked the few yards from her car to her office, Marla was still in such a perturbed state that she never even noticed the blond woman watching her from across the street.

Jack was framing one of his pictures when Claire came back from her lunch hour. As usual, she brought him a sandwich from the restaurant on Second Street. He stopped his work and cleared off a spot on the table with its jumble of paints and brushes. Pulling up a nearby straight-back wood chair, he sat down to eat. "Ham and cheese," he said, opening the wrapping paper. "Good."

Claire brought him a cup of coffee to have with it. It was nice of her to cater to him the way she did, but sometimes her hovering became a little annoying, especially when he was trying to work. He didn't mind at the moment, though. Marla had worked late last night and gotten up early to go to her office that morning, so it was nice to have someone to talk to while he had lunch.

"Thanks," he said when she had set the coffee in front of him. "How are things in the big city?"

"Seattle?" she said.

"No, I meant Langley." Jack smiled at her confusion. Claire's sense of humor tended to be a little slow.

"Oh, I see. Langley's so small." She chuckled now that she had gotten his little joke. Her smile faded then. "Well," she said, sighing, "even in a small town things happen that aren't so pleasant."

Jack finished chewing a bite of sandwich. "Oh? Like what? The restaurant found a dead mouse in the kitchen?"

She smiled again briefly. "No. I'm sorry to be the one to tell you this, but . . . I think it's best that you know, and that you hear it from a friend who has your best interests at heart."

Jack sipped his coffee and looked at Claire curiously. Her words seemed a little rehearsed, but she appeared genuinely concerned about something as she leaned against the table in her pastel green skirt and sweater. "What are you talking about?"

Claire bowed her head slightly. "Marla, I'm afraid."

He set down his coffee mug. "Marla?"

"Yes. I was coming out of the restaurant when I saw her pull up in front of her office. There was a man in her car. He was . . . well, about her age, I would guess, and . . . very good-looking."

Jack was growing uneasy. He didn't like the way Claire

133

was taking so much time getting to the point. "He was probably some buyer she's working with."

Claire lifted her head and took a long breath. "He may be; I don't know. What I do know is—I hate to tell you this because I know it will hurt you, but—they were kissing in the car."

Jack stared at her blankly for a moment. "What do you mean?" It wasn't true. It couldn't be.

Claire made a helpless gesture with her small hands. "They kissed each other, Jack. On the mouth. I saw it with my own eyes. I know how much you think of her, but I could have predicted something like this would happen. It's just as I told you before you married her. She's not worthy of you."

"I don't believe it!" A sick emptiness gripped his stomach, and he felt numb. It couldn't be true. Marla wouldn't do that to him, not now. Not after what they'd shared together the last two months.

"Jack, why would I lie? We've been friends for years, you and Harry and I. Have you ever known me to lie about someone? I wouldn't have told you about it at all, knowing how the news would upset you, but I decided the sooner you knew, the less painful it would be for you. I'm just sad to have to be the one to tell you. I'm sorry you ever married her."

"That's why you're saying this. You're jealous of her!" he accused, his tone aggressive. "You never wanted me to marry her, and you're saying this out of spite!"

Claire looked deeply wounded. "Jack, you're imagining things. Why should I be jealous of someone like her? The only reason I thought you shouldn't marry her is that I was afraid she would do something exactly like this. I'm sorry that my advice was proved right, but you don't have to blame me for it."

Jack was quiet now, trying to think, trying to find a way to make it not true. His stomach was beginning to churn.

"Tell me again exactly what you saw," he said in a less reproachful tone.

"They drove up in the car together," she said, not at all reticent to repeat the story. "This man leaned toward her, put his arms around her and they kissed. He hurried out of the car then and walked off. I suppose they were afraid someone might see them together and that was why he rushed away. Marla got out of the car then and went into her office."

Jack pushed away his partly eaten sandwich. Looking at it made him nauseous now. "Would you leave me alone for a while, Claire?" he said, his voice hoarse.

"Of course, Jack," she said sympathetically. She put her hand on his shoulder for a moment, then quietly walked out of the studio.

Jack buried his face in his hands as tears came to his eyes. *Oh, God, how could it be true? Why would she need someone else?* He'd thought they had so much together. Wasn't it enough? Wasn't *he* enough for her? Without his even realizing it, was she losing interest in him already? Didn't she love him?

With an impatient hand he brushed away the wetness under his eyes. *Was Claire making it up?* he asked himself, trying to think it through logically. No, he didn't believe she was. She might gloat over the truth, but she wouldn't have made up a story like that. She wasn't the type to lie.

Feeling wretched, he got up from the table and began to pace unsteadily about the room. Why would Marla have kissed some man? Had she been showing him homes? Maybe he wasn't a buyer. Was it Devin? No, it couldn't be. Whatever Marla had felt, Jack knew for sure how attached Devin was to Ginger. He remembered their wedding. Devin's loving gazes at his wife were the final proof that he had never been involved with Marla. And now that Ginger was pregnant . . .

No, it certainly wasn't Devin. But who? Someone good-looking and about Marla's age, Claire had said. Jack shook his head. It must be some man she had met on her job. Was what he had once thought true—that any man could turn her head?

Jack went to the window and leaned against the frame for support. He felt weak and physically ill. His head was swimming. What should he do? How could he stop her from going after others? She had actually let another man *kiss* her! Was there even more to it? Were they having an affair? The man had rushed off, Claire had said, as though he didn't want to be seen with her. They must be hiding something. How long had it been going on?

A tear coursed down Jack's gaunt cheek. He raked his hands through his hair. She was always so passionate when they made love together, Jack thought. Since their wedding, she'd seemed so devoted. How could she be so false?

Maybe there was some explanation. Maybe Claire had somehow misinterpreted what she saw. He wouldn't confront Marla with what he'd learned; not yet. Having been wrong in the past, he'd better be sure this time. But if she was being unfaithful—oh, God—what would he do? He loved her so much.

When he got home that evening, Marla wasn't there. For the first time since their wedding, he wondered where she was. His tears had subsided hours ago, and he was bitter and methodical now. He'd call her at her office to see if she was actually there.

When she answered the phone he was relieved, but his confidence was far from restored. "I was just wondering how late you'll be," he said.

"Another half-hour or so. I'm finishing up some paperwork," she said in that soft voice she saved for him. At least he had always thought she spoke only to him that way.

"All right," he said. "I'll put some steaks on."

When she got home she seemed tired and ready to relax,

just the way she had been coming home since they'd married. She enjoyed the dinner Jack had prepared, but she soon seemed to notice his coolness. He was trying to act normal but found it difficult.

"How did things go at the gallery today?" she asked as they sat down together on the living room couch after dinner. Max was curled up on a nearby chair. "Some problem came up?"

"No."

"You're just tired? Is that why you're so quiet?" She stroked his cheek, then ruffled her fingers through his hair.

The gentle, caring gesture made goose bumps rise on his back. He loved her touch. "I guess so," he said, a distance in his voice as he answered her question.

"Guess so? Don't you know?" she teased.

Jack made a grim little smile, then backed away from her fingers tickling his ear.

She drew her hand away. "What's wrong?" Her tone was more serious now. "Are you angry about something?"

"No." He kept his eyes fixed straight ahead.

She was silent for a moment. "I haven't seen you act like this since . . . Are you upset because I've been working late so much?"

"No," he said, impatient now, wishing she'd quit questioning him. He didn't want to talk about it. But he realized it was his stiff behavior that was provoking her questions. Trying to make himself relax, he smiled. "I guess I am kind of tired tonight."

She nodded her head and leaned back, apparently accepting his excuse. Taking his hand in hers, she fondled it. "Maybe we should go to bed early then."

Jack felt cold suddenly. Her voice had that let's-make-love quality. He didn't want to. How could he, knowing another man had had his arms around her that very day? He said nothing.

"Jack?" She leaned toward him and ran her hand up his

chest. After kissing his cheek, she whispered, "Why don't we make love? It'll perk up your spirits."

His eyes closed in pain and he didn't answer.

"Don't you feel well?" she asked, sounding very concerned now.

"I'm fine," he insisted. "Just . . . tired."

She smiled and began to unbutton his shirt. "Too tired to make love?" she cajoled.

"You never are, are you?" he said, keeping his voice even.

"No," she said, her voice like honey. "Never too tired."

His shirt was unbuttoned now and she ran her hand over his bared chest, pausing at his nipple, caressing it with her fingertips. It made Jack's breath come quicker. He couldn't prevent his own arousal. Even the suspicion that she was unfaithful couldn't keep him inured to her. It made him angry. How could he be so weak that he would still want her no matter what she had done?

She unbuckled his belt and unzipped his pants. Her hand slid confidently beneath, feeling him. "You see?" she said, laughing lightly as she nuzzled her nose against his neck. "You're not too tired at all!"

Jack's jaw clenched tightly. Marla was always so sure of herself. She crooked her finger and knew her trusting husband would be right there, like a panting puppy.

His expression was grim and calculating for a moment. Well, then, maybe he'd better give her what she wanted, he thought. He put his arms around her. But as she brought her lips up to his to kiss him, he turned his face away. No, he wouldn't kiss her. He wouldn't touch the lips another man had touched. Instead he swiftly picked her up in his arms and carried her into their bedroom.

In moments he had undressed himself. Roughly he removed Marla's clothes as she lay on the bed where he had put her. "Jack!" she said, smiling with surprise as he tugged off her panties, leaving her naked. "You've turned from a lamb into a bull in a few minutes!"

"Just trying to keep my wife happy." A trace of sarcasm tinged his voice as he eased himself down next to her. "Keeping you satisfied is a full-time job."

A shadow crossed her eyes. "You never seem to mind it," she said, her smile hesitant.

"Oh, no," he assured her. His voice was softly aggressive now. "Not in the least. Trying to find your saturation point has been a pleasant enough chore. I mean to keep trying until we reach it."

She smiled and looked at him. "You're in an odd mood tonight. I've never seen you like this."

"And the night isn't even over," he said sardonically. He ran his hand over her smooth body, from her flat stomach upward over her soft breasts. Her body looked so innocent and unprotected, he thought as he rubbed her nipples into little peaks with his fingertips. Mentally she was always so strong and confident, but her body was only a soft, vulnerable woman's. Did she understand, he wondered, how helpless she really was at this moment? Did she ever stop to consider how much stronger physically he was than she? He could threaten her and make her be faithful, if he wanted to. He could show her who was boss, so she wouldn't dare even to look at another man.

But that wasn't his way. No matter what she did, he could never harm her. If she didn't stay with him by choice, there was no purpose in their relationship.

But she *had* chosen him for her husband two months ago. Was she so wanton that being with one man for even that short a time was too restricting? How arduously and often did she have to be made love to to keep her from roaming to other men? Or did she simply need variety?

"Oh, Jack," she murmured. Her eyes were closed and her lips softened in pleasure as he continued to caress her swelling breasts.

"Do you like that?" he said.

"Oh, yes." Her voice was laden with sensuality.

Oh, yes, she always did, Jack thought as he brought his hand down to her thighs. He'd never met a woman who was so sexually eager and quick to respond. As if to prove it, he slipped his hand between her warm thighs to touch her hidden femininity. Already she was smooth and moist and ready for him.

She gasped sharply at his touch and parted her thighs. Her body writhed in that graceful, sexy way of hers that never failed to arouse him to heated urgency. He loved to watch her respond to him. It always made him feel confident and secure in his masculinity. No wonder other men wanted her. They could sense that pleasing a woman like Marla would make them feel powerful and virile.

In spite of his doubts, he felt that way himself now as he moved over her. She put her arms around him, and he let her draw him to her. Sliding gently between her thighs, he slowly penetrated her eager body. She felt warm and firm as his manhood became enclosed within her. Maybe he was wrong; maybe it was women who had all the power during sex, he thought fleetingly. He was growing drunk on the feel of her pulsating, soft body that had him captured in such sweet agony.

It was too much for him. Profound need drove him to press her hard into the bedcovers, thrusting until, just as she clutched him and cried out in fulfillment, the burst of his own passion came like a giant star fall.

He lay still for a moment, feeling her slender, supple frame relax beneath him. He moved off her then and lay at her side. Turning his head on the pillow to look at her, he saw her lying in a languid pose, one knee bent, one arm over her waist, limp and warm. Her beautiful eyes were closed, her hair mussed, and her expression was dreamy.

As he gazed at her, her eyes opened, dark and shining. "Mmmm, that was nice," she said, her voice a rich whisper.

"Was it?" he asked softly.

She turned her body toward him and put her hand on his

140

chest. "Didn't you think so?" she said cozily, laying her head on his shoulder.

"You always make me happy, Marla." His voice was a little sad, but she didn't seem to notice. He could tell she was growing sleepy. She was obviously content now, but for how long? Tomorrow, if her handsome friend came back, would she need the excitement of his kisses again? Would she crave even more?

Jack's expression grew troubled and morose as he lay there, his wife sleeping against his shoulder. He made no effort to touch or stroke her as he usually did. Feeling her gentle weight against him, he could only wonder what tomorrow would bring.

After a few minutes of forlorn speculation, he grew angry at his seeming helplessness in the situation. There must be something he could do to keep her from others. He was damned if he was going to passively let her do as she pleased! He couldn't lock her in the house; but if he could wear her down enough, maybe she wouldn't have the energy to wander off behind his back. His taunt earlier about finding her saturation point came to his mind. What did he have to lose?

Jaws tightening as he repressed his bitterness, he reached to touch her breast. After fondling the soft mound of flesh, he moved his hands firmly over her body, massaging and caressing her until she opened her eyes again.

She smiled sleepily. "Jack, what are you doing?" Her voice was groggy.

"Don't you want more?"

Hesitating, she rubbed her eyes. "If you do," she said.

She looked like she was a little tired for sex just now, Jack thought. Good. When he was finished she would be so exhausted, she wouldn't know her own name. And then maybe she'd lose interest in her friend's adulterous advances.

"I do," Jack said. "I want you again." He slid his hand between her thighs and slowly began to stimulate her. She was unresponsive for a moment, and then the familiar soft smile came over her face.

"Are you trying to relive our honeymoon?" she asked with a chuckle.

"Why not?" he said, keeping his voice light.

"I had more energy then. I hadn't spent all day working," she said, her breath beginning to quicken.

Working, or making love with someone else? Jack thought with pain. He blinked back the burning sensation in his eyes and swallowed back revulsion at the image his question had brought to mind. Marla, his wife, allowing another man to touch her intimately, the way he was now—the thought made him wild. He had to blot it out.

Jack shut his eyes and concentrated on the present. He opened his eyes again at her soft moan. Her body was growing restless under his insistent handling. Bending over her, he bit and licked each nipple in turn, making her gasp. She squirmed against him and stroked his chest with his small hands, then reached below to caress him. It wasn't long before he needed her body again as much as he had made her want him once more. But he made himself hold back. This time he would not let himself go until she was completely spent. His purpose was to sate her, not to demonstrate his love. *Why did it have to come to this,* he thought. His eyes burned again with hot tears that rose beneath his lids.

Reining in his resentment, keeping his hands gentle, he made them one, his chest against her back. He closed his eyes and tried to repress the stunning sensation he always received when he entered her special feminine place.

She gasped in delight. He could tell she was wide awake now. Fine. He wouldn't want her to sleep through this. He continued the undulation of his pelvis in unison with hers and he began to caress her breasts.

"Oh, darling, this is wonderful," she whispered. Her breathing was growing ragged now. He took it as a cue to quicken his thrusts and caress her more fervently, all the while keeping himself from becoming overinvolved. If he did, it would defeat his purpose. He had to outlast her.

"Oh, Jack! Oh . . ." Her voice had a frenzied quality to it. A small smile of satisfaction came over his face. In another moment . . .

All at once she made a high, sharp cry. Her body rocked convulsively against him. Jack held his breath through it, squeezing his eyes shut. When she stopped and her body relaxed, he breathed out a long, silent sigh. It was over, and he had managed to keep his own body in check. Beads of perspiration gave a sheen to his forehead. It was beginning to be something of an ordeal for him, but he wasn't through yet.

After only a moment to let her recover, he began to stimulate her again. She stopped his hand. "Oh, no. No more," she said weakly.

"But I still need you." He knew she must feel his as yet unleashed power within her.

"I know," she said. "Go ahead, darling, but you don't have to touch me anymore. I've had enough." He could hear the satisfaction in her voice.

Saying nothing, he began his thrusting movements again, more gently now. He continued to caress her breasts, and after a few moments he edged his fingers between her thighs again. She grabbed his wrist to try to stop him. "No, Jack. It's too much."

He ignored her, taking advantage, for once, of his superior strength.

"Jack, please . . . it's too . . . sensitive . . ." Gradually the tone of her voice began to change, and her tight grip on his wrist loosened. "Ohhh," she said in a long sigh. A moment later she took a deep breath—and didn't release it.

"Marla?"

"Oh . . . Jack . . ." There was awe in her hushed voice as she finally exhaled. She seemed to grow lax against him for several moments, then her muscles tightened again.

143

"Jack, oh Jack," she repeated softly, like an incantation. He had never seen her respond quite like this before.

"Are you okay?" he asked.

She was silent.

"Marla?"

He rose up slightly to glimpse her face. Her eyes were shut tight and her mouth was parted. Her breathing was shallow.

"Do you want me to stop?" he asked. He was growing concerned now about what was happening to her.

"No!" Her breaths were suddenly husky. "Oh, God, no. Please, darling . . . more . . ."

Reluctantly he deepened his thrusts and quickened the stimulating movement of his hand. Her reaction was low, shuddering gasps that almost sounded like sobs. It was beginning to frighten him. He didn't know what he was doing to her, and he wanted to stop.

"Don't stop!" she cried, as though she had sensed his thought. "Don't stop! Please, don't stop! Please don't . . ."

Jack renewed his efforts, his own breathing heavy and uneven now. A drop of sweat ran down his cheek. The stimulation he was giving her was growing too much for his resistance. Her profound responses made him anxious and alert as he had never been before.

He was moving against her as hard as he dared now without physically injuring her. "Oh, Jack!" she cried out and reached to grip the edge of the mattress. The bed covers were bundled in her taut, clenched hand.

All at once she was still as death for an instant, and then she gasped and cried out his name in a wrenching moan. Her slender body was suddenly quaking in his arms, shaking against him violently. He let go then himself, barely realizing it until the heat of passion swept him into a giant fire fall, a glowing star burst much more vivid and intense than he had ever known.

He was fighting for breath in the next moment, his heart pounding as if he had just run ten miles. When he regained his senses, he drew away from Marla a bit and looked down at her. Her body felt limp as he shifted her position and let her lie on the bed covers. Her breathing was very shallow, and her eyes were closed as if in sleep. A dewy glaze covered her body.

"Marla?" He shook her a bit, but she didn't respond. *Was she unconscious?* he wondered, feeling cold with sudden apprehension. "Marla!" He lightly tapped her cheeks.

Her dark eyes fluttered open, as if in surprise. Jack sank down beside her in relief. "Are you all right?" he asked, touching her hand as she rubbed her palms over her face.

She was smiling weakly, exhausted, when she pulled her hands away. "I'm fine," she half-whispered, a little breathless. "Oh, Jack!" Reaching up lightly, she stroked his cheek and chin. "You were magnificent! I never dreamed it could be like that. How did you know?" Her lustrous eyes gazed into his in wonder. "I didn't think I wanted any more. But you made me go on, and it was so thrilling! Was it for you, too?" Her voice was filled with dazed admiration. Jack didn't know what to say, except to nod his head that, yes, it was a thrill for him, too. Like riding a roller coaster without seat belts in the dark.

She cuddled up warmly against him as he lay back on the pillow, his energy totally spent. He put his arms around her, not quite sure what to think of her, himself or anything at that moment. His head was still spinning.

"Oh, darling," she whispered eagerly in the quiet stillness of their bedroom. "You're so virile. You're a marvelous lover. I bet there's no other man in the world like you." She sounded almost like a child now, who'd just received a wonderful present. "I'm so lucky to be married to you. I love you."

A tear slid from his eyes as he listened to her praise. His ignoble intention had been not to love her but to satiate her. And somehow it had brought on what seemed like near-worship from his wife. He bent his head forward to kiss the top of her head. "I love you, too," he murmured.

He lay back then and blinked his moist eyes. Where was he now? He'd never expected all this from the wife he thought was being unfaithful to him. Was Claire wrong? Were his own perceptions wrong? Had he hallucinated the last several minutes of soul-shaking passion with Marla? Was he imagining her admiration because it was what he wanted to hear?

He looked down at her, sleeping meekly in his arms. She was real enough. And their lovemaking had been real, too. Jack felt very confused.

CHAPTER EIGHT

Marla was as bright and lighthearted as a canary the next morning as she drove to work. She felt buoyant, full of life and health, the pleasant residue from Jack's lovemaking the night before. She had always deeply enjoyed going to bed with him, but last night was like being hurled onto Mount Olympus, where the gods played. Jack was becoming such an expert lover, she didn't know if she would be able to keep up with him. *But it would be fun trying!* she thought with a smile as she turned onto Second Street. It was odd that he had been so quiet this morning, as if he didn't know what to say. He had been like that last night, too, when their physical fireworks were over. Were all great lovers so shy afterward?

She chuckled at the question as she parked her car in front of her office. Her delightful disposition faltered when she saw through the large display window that Rory Preston was already in the office, waiting at her desk. The secretary had obviously let him in.

"Hello!" he said in a speculative way when he saw her come in. "You look like you're in a cheerful mood. Until you walked in, anyway."

She nodded vaguely. How could she even be polite to him? Should she tell him to leave, get himself another realtor?

"I'd like to go take another look at that house again," he

said. "As I was considering the whole thing last night, I realized I hadn't checked the landscaping very well."

"All right," she said, sighing. Asking him to go elsewhere didn't mean he would. She'd already tried that once. But if she sold him the house, he wouldn't have any excuse to come around anymore. "But you'd better behave yourself!" she warned.

"Sure!" he replied.

On the way he asked innocuous questions about her background. Upon learning that her maiden name was Rosetti, he said, "Italian, eh? I'm half French, on my mother's side. I thought we had something in common—we both have that passionate Mediterranean blood in our veins." Marla ignored him.

They arrived at the house and Preston spent some time walking over the property, commenting on the landscaping and the small size of the lot. Marla did her best to point out the home's advantages, noting how close it was to the beach. They went inside the house again to look it over once more.

"It'll need a new paint job," he said. "You can see where the pictures were hanging." He pointed to rectangular gray outlines on the living room walls.

"You can note that when you make your offer—use it as one of your reasons for lowering the asking price," Marla said.

Preston nodded and continued looking around.

"Shall we write it up?" she asked, pressing him a bit.

"My offer?" He smiled. "I knew you could be an aggressive saleswoman if you wanted to be. I wish you were a little more aggressive in other ways, too." He was looking directly at her now, his eyes glistening with ideas. "You're a woman I'd definitely like to know better."

"Mr. Preston . . ."

"Rory."

"I thought I made it clear last time that my only interest in dealing with you is at the business level."

"You did. But I think that was just a bluff," he said with confidence.

"I'm happily married," she said, growing annoyed.

"So? That doesn't bother me," he said with a grin.

"It does me!" Anger clipped her words.

"It shouldn't," he replied easily. "Your husband doesn't have to know. What's a little fling here or there? Variety's the spice of life. *La dolce vita!*"

"My marriage is very important to me, and I don't intend to carry this conversation any further," she told him in an iron-firm voice.

He quickly walked over to her and put his arm around her shoulders. She tried to move away, but he walked along with her and hung on. "Look, baby, I understand you want to stay married. That's fine with me. I'm just looking for a little extracurricular activity, you know?"

"Well, I'm not!" She removed his hand from her shoulder and walked away.

"I'm good. You wouldn't regret it," he said.

Marla chuckled softly, sublimely amused at the man's ego. "My husband's worth ten of you! Not interested; sorry." The cockiness of her words came from conviction. After last night she was certain no one could compare with Jack.

His expression soured. "You're sure haughty all of a sudden!"

"Having a husband like mine, I have a lot to be haughty about," she said.

"I'm getting pretty sick of hearing about your husband."

"Why don't we get back to talking about the house then?" she said. "It's what we're here for."

"You want to sell me this house?" His tone was getting ugly now.

"Yes."

"How badly?"

"Not that badly," she said with cool sarcasm.

"Let's forget it, then," he said, moving briskly toward the open front door.

"All right," she said breezily. She walked behind him toward the door, getting out her car keys. The sale didn't matter to her in the least. She just wanted to be rid of him one way or another.

At the door he stopped abruptly and turned. Before she knew it, she was in his arms again. Her reflexes were quicker this time. She managed to get one hand planted firmly against his chest. The other she poised at the bottom of his throat, her car keys sticking up like two jagged teeth from her knuckled fist, ready to thrust upward against his Adam's apple, if necessary.

He saw his situation and laughed snidely. "God, you're a spitfire! I'd love to get you in bed."

"When hell freezes over," she said. With one quick effort that took all her strength, she pushed herself out of his hold. It left her slightly out of breath.

"You're too all-fire sure of yourself, you know that?" he said, shrugging his shoulders to straighten his jacket, as if trying to get back his male dignity.

"Your opinion doesn't concern me at all." She moved past him out of the house.

He followed. "Someone ought to teach you a lesson," he said, a little too quietly.

Marla paused to lock the door. "It won't be you." Briskly she walked to her car without giving him so much as a glance. She had had more than enough.

She got behind the steering wheel. Preston got in on the passenger side a second later, as she was starting the motor. It was a shame he was so quick, she thought. She had been ready to drive off and leave him there. Her heart was pounding, both from dodging his advances and from anger. And, she had to admit, from an ounce of apprehension. Never before had she had to deal with a man who was so sexually aggressive.

Preston was quiet for a long while, seemingly passive as he watched the farm pastures and patches of forest go past out the window once they had gotten out of the residential area. Marla grew calmer, too, though she was far from at ease.

At last he said, "What's this husband of yours like? Italian, too?"

"No, he's a handsome blond Anglo-Saxon," she said with pride.

"Blue eyes?" he said, sounding disgusted.

"Yes!" Marla said with a smile.

"What does he do?"

"He's an artist."

Preston started laughing. "You're bowled over by some pale, Milquetoast artist? Why don't you see what a real man is like?"

Marla took a deep breath. "Jack will do for me," she said with a secure timbre in her voice.

"He'll do? Look, honey, I'd be happy to demonstrate what you're missing."

"You try it and I'll kick you in your antipasto!"

He looked at her sharply a moment, then laughed grudgingly. There was a certain respect in his voice as he said, "You're tough, but I like you. Too bad you have that weakness for blond wimps. But I suppose he must bring in some bucks, considering that ring he gave you. Can't blame you for wanting to stick with that."

They were arriving in Langley now, and she was hardly listening to Preston anymore. She was thinking ahead as to how to get out of the car fast enough so he wouldn't be able to make another pass at her as he had the last time she brought him back to the office. As she drove along Anthes Avenue, she saw Jack coming out of the bank on the corner of Anthes and Second Street, where he regularly did business. He paused as he saw her white car go past. Disconcerted as she was about handling Preston, she only gave Jack a quick wave, then turned the corner and pulled up in front of her office in the middle of the block.

"Was that him?" Preston asked.

He had to wait for his answer, because Marla didn't waste a split second getting out of the car. She was stepping onto the sidewalk as he exited the passenger side. "Yes, that was him," she said quietly. "So I take it you've lost interest in the house?"

Preston was looking up the street. Marla turned and could see Jack walking up Anthes toward First, his tall, lanky figure masculine and very sexy, she thought, in blue jeans and one of his work shirts. His blond hair caught the sunlight. In a moment Jack was out of view because of the corner buildings.

"He looks a little thin," Preston said.

"Muscles never impressed me much," Marla replied. She flicked a dismissive glance at Preston's biceps, which bulged his jacket sleeves.

"Is that so?"

"Sorry," she said. "About the house . . ."

"I'm still thinking about it. I'll let you know."

"Okay. I won't hold my breath." She turned and went into her office, leaving him there on the sidewalk. Through the window Marla watched him walk to his car across the street in a skulking manner. She heaved a sigh, relieved to see him drive away.

"I hope that's the last I see of him," she told Maggie an hour or so later, after filling her co-worker in on what had happened. Maggie had returned from showing a new potential buyer some homes and had asked Marla about Preston.

"I hope so, too," Maggie said, looking concerned. She was gathering several papers together on her desk. "He sounds a little dangerous, if you ask me."

"Oh, I can handle him," Marla said, not wanting her friend to worry. But she didn't feel as sure of herself as her words indicated.

"If he does come back, I wouldn't go out to that vacant house alone with him again," Maggie said. "I've heard of incidents happening to real estate women in situations like that. After the way he foisted himself on you in the car yesterday, I wouldn't have gone out alone with him today."

"It's part of the job," Marla said fatalistically. "It's one reason I'm beginning to dislike this work."

"You should have asked one of us to go with you this morning. I would have gone," Maggie said, reaching across her desk for her stapler.

"And then you would have missed your opportunity to help your new buyer who came in later. Don't be silly. I can take care of myself."

"Well, I just hope he doesn't show up again!" Maggie stapled her papers together with a finality that made Marla smile. It was good to have friends who cared, she thought.

Jack was unusually quiet as they sat at the dining room table that evening. He had chased Max away with a sound whack of his hand when the cat jumped onto the table and nosed the casserole they were eating. Marla had made and frozen it a few weeks ago. She was pleased that it tasted so good after being reheated in the oven, but Jack had made no comment about it one way or another. He wasn't eating much of it, either.

"Don't you like it?" she asked.

"It's fine," he said absently, poking at the food with his fork.

"Do you feel all right?"

"Fine."

"How are things at work?"

"Fine," he replied, growing annoyed.

"You've been so quiet lately, I was just wondering—"

"How was your day?" he interrupted, not looking at her.

"Oh, okay," she said with a sigh. "Still busy."

"New client this morning?" he asked.

153

She looked at him blankly a moment, then remembered he had seen her pass in the car on the way back to the office. "Yes, I've been working with him for a few days."

"He's looking for a home?" Jack sounded strangely disinterested, but Marla didn't stop to think about her husband's odd manner, figuring he must be tired again.

"Yes, among other things," she said sardonically.

"What does that mean?" Jack was looking at her now.

Marla hesitated. "Maybe you can give me some advice. He's—been making passes at me. It's getting so that I'm not entirely sure I can handle him."

"You aren't?" Jack's tone was clipped and his eyes bright with accusation as he steadily stared at her. It took Marla totally off-guard.

"No," she said uncertainly, not understanding Jack's reaction. "He's gotten pretty aggressive."

"And what have you been doing to spur him on?" Jack said.

Marla's eyes widened a bit. She slowly put down her fork. "Nothing."

"Oh, come on!" Jack said derisively.

"I haven't done anything. In fact, I've done all I can to keep him in line."

"If that were true, you wouldn't be having any trouble with him," Jack said, his words absolute.

Marla was astounded by his attitude. "How can you say that?"

"Because a man doesn't make passes at a woman unless he thinks his advances will be welcomed."

Marla gaped at him for a moment. "When a woman gets raped, do you automatically figure it must have been her fault, too?"

Jack sighed and looked disgusted. "No. But we aren't talking about rape here, are we, Marla? We're talking about a man you're working with who's apparently decided you're hot stuff. That's why he's after you, isn't it? He wouldn't think you're so hot if you weren't making yourself look available. If you were that bothered by his advances, you would have told him to find another agent."

"That's not how I do business! I can't just dump every buyer who annoys me. How dare you say that I've been leading him on!" Marla all but spit the words at him.

Jack's face reddened, and she could see the veins sticking out in his throat. "I know you well enough to say anything I please," he said. "When I asked you to sleep with me on our second date, do you think I had much doubt that you'd say yes? After I stopped seeing you because you were chasing Devin, look at the way you went after me. You stopped at nothing—tricks, seductive clothes, baring your body—to get me back. Now you're insulted because I assume you must have done something to lead this guy on. Do you think I'm stupid, Marla? You're insulting my intelligence!"

Marla felt as if she had just been knocked across the room. She grew pale as she sat in her seat and stared at him across the table. Vaguely, from the corner of her eye, she saw a white streak as Maxie fled the room. "I can't believe you're . . ." she began, her voice faltering. She swallowed and tried to compose herself. "Why do you think that the way I've behaved with you is the way I act with every man? I'm in *love* with you. Maybe some of the things I did were foolish, but it was because I loved you and wanted you. I wouldn't behave that way with anyone else."

"Then why did you let this guy kiss you?" Jack retorted.

Marla's mind jogged. She stared at him. "How do you know he kissed me?"

"Because someone saw you two in your car yesterday morning." He glared at her, as if waiting for her to deny it.

"Who saw it?"

"What difference does it make? Are you going to tell me it's not true?" he challenged.

"He took me by surprise and forced himself on me," she explained. "I didn't *want* to kiss him! I pushed him away."

Her dark eyes showed all the earnestness the innocent truth could lend.

A flicker of uncertainty passed through Jack's eyes, but it lasted only an instant. "You're always such a good actress—and so clever with excuses."

"I'm telling the truth!" She opened the palm of her hand, as if begging for him to be reasonable. "Didn't I just ask you for advice about handling this man a few minutes ago?"

Jack chuckled in mocking amusement. "You've always been so expert at handling men, I don't know why you'd need *my* advice. Besides, you know I saw you two together this morning. Maybe you just asked me that question to set up a smoke screen."

Marla felt bitterness cutting through her at his blind, un-compromising attitude. It was an ugly feeling and it tore her apart, but there it was. "I asked you because I hoped you might give me some clues as to how men think. But I can see now you've all got rocks in your head! I tell him I'm not interested and he doesn't pay any attention. I tell you I don't do anything to lead men on and you don't believe me. Why is it you men always stick together? Do you realize you're defending him against me? It's not *his* fault, because *I'm* leading him on—that's what you've said. Isn't anything ever a *man's* fault?"

Jack took his napkin from his lap and threw it onto the table over his half-eaten dinner. "I don't feel like discussing this with you." He got up from the table.

Marla followed him into the living room. "Why?" she demanded.

"Because you're talking nonsense!"

"I'm trying to make you see that what you're saying isn't logical." She came up beside him as he stood at the front window, looking out onto the street through the sheer curtains.

"Women don't have any logic. They just know how to

wrap a man around their finger and keep him bobbing like a yo-yo." Jack's voice had grown tired and cold.

"Maybe that's why you don't know up from down!" she said. "And who saw him kiss me?"

Jack sighed. "Claire."

Marla gritted her teeth. "Claire. I should have guessed!"

Jack turned from the window toward her. "You haven't denied kissing him. What difference does it make if it was Claire or someone else who saw it?"

"Because Claire isn't an impartial observer. Is that what she told you, that *I* kissed Preston? *He* kissed me—and I pushed him away! There's a big difference in how the story's told."

"Preston? Is that his name?"

"Yes, Rory Preston. What does it matter?" she said, impatient. Jack was obviously ignoring her point.

"I might as well know who's having an affair with my wife," Jack said coldly, turning toward the window again.

"Affair!"

"Claire said he got out of the car quickly, as if you were afraid of being seen together. Even this morning you drove right past me. It's pretty clear you're hiding something."

Marla was so incensed, she had to grab onto the heavy window drape to steady herself. "He got out of the car fast because I was trying to slap him!"

Jack looked at her and almost laughed in her face. "Slap him? And he—that big guy—was so scared of you, he ran out of the car? Then, after such an altercation, you still went out with him again today, ready for more? Come on, Marla, I've heard you come up with better stories than that."

"He . . ." She stammered and then realized there was nothing she could say to explain what the true situation was. Nothing he would believe, anyway. "Jack," she finally said, her eyes begging for reason, "remember how we made love together last night? After that, how can you believe I could be untrue to you?"

Jack's face was suddenly expressionless and pale. "I wasn't making love last night, Marla. Claire had already told me about you and this Preston fellow. I didn't even want to kiss you, knowing he had. You wanted sex, so I complied. Actually it was a little test. I wanted to see if I could burn you out—if you had some limit I could reach so you wouldn't want to go to other men. Seeing you with him this morning, I knew I had failed."

Marla felt faint for a moment. How could it be true? That beautiful night of love was just a sham? "You did make love to me last night," she insisted, tears blinding her. "You said you loved me. You did! And Rory Preston is just one of my buyers. Maybe I should have sent him away, but I was just trying to do my job. I showed him a home today, that's all."

Jack shook his head. "If he was middle-aged and paunchy, I might believe that. But I got a good look at him when you passed by in the car. He looks like a muscle-bound sex machine. Just what you need, I suppose. Even Claire called him handsome."

"Claire! She's the one who planted all these ideas in your head! Don't you see, she wants to break us up so she can marry you herself? Why do you believe her version of all this and not mine?"

Jack sighed and made an empty gesture with his hand. "You wanted me to be logical, Marla. Knowing you and how you've behaved with men in the past, her story simply makes more sense. And in all the years I've known Claire, she's never lied or been deceitful. I wish I could say the same for you."

Marla angrily wiped away the hot tears that were flowing down her cheeks. "So now you see me as some sort of slut again, is that it?"

Jack's eyes misted, and he stared out the window again as if with unseeing eyes. "I don't know what you are. All I know is, for some reason I'm not happy without you. I wish I could get you out of my system and just go back to the way

I was before I met you. But I tried that once and I couldn't do it. When you came back, saying you wanted me, even though I tried to resist, I was putty in your hands. I still am. Even when I don't want you, like last night, I still want you. It's not love, I don't think. It's some sort of sexual addiction. You have something all men want. If I have to stand in line like the rest of them, I suppose that's what I'll do. I've even lost all pride, telling you I'll be here waiting when you come back from your little forays, knowing you've broken the promise you made to be faithful." He was silent and grim for several moments as he stared out the window. He turned toward her then, his eyes deeply melancholy. "Well, you know where I stand now," he said quietly, as if resigned to fate. "You win on all counts. No doubt you always will."

"Well, *I* won't be here, Jack!" she said after listening to him. "*I* have more pride than to stay with a husband who thinks I'm one step above a whore, who says he doesn't even love me! I'm not going to wait around for you to come to your senses. If you trust Claire so much, you should have married *her!*"

She walked around him and went straight to the bedroom. Going to the closet, she took down a large suitcase. She set it on the bed, opened it, then slid her drawer of underwear from her dresser, turned it over and dumped the contents in. She went back to the closet next, pulled blouses, skirts and dresses off their hangers and tossed them into the suitcase in a colorful flurry of flying clothes.

"What are you doing?" Jack asked, watching from the doorway.

"Leaving you," she said.

"Wait," he said, stepping in to shut the lid of the suitcase so she couldn't throw in any more clothes. "I didn't say I wanted you to leave."

"I don't care what you want. I'm going!"

"Marla," he said, fighting with her as she tried to open the suitcase again, "we can try to work this out. Maybe we can see a counselor. Whatever problems there are, I don't want you out of my life. I told you, I'm not happy without you."

"You're not happy *with* me, either. And I'm not happy with you thinking I'm being unfaithful all the time. I don't see any use in us trying to go on together. Let go of my suitcase!"

He did as she demanded. As he watched, she threw in more clothes, tucking in the ends of the jumble of materials. "Where will you go?" he asked, sounding angry now.

"I don't know. I'll think of something."

"It's dark out already," he protested.

"Then I'll be in my element. Don't streetwalkers do most of their business at night?"

"Marla!" he snapped at her, sounding at his wit's end now.

She pushed hard on the suitcase lid, trying to close it. Finally she managed to press its latches shut. She lifted it off the bed and began to walk out. Jack blocked her way at the door.

"Don't do this," he said. "Try to be reasonable!"

"Me be reasonable! How about you?"

"I am," he said hotly. "Can't you see that? I know better than to try to change you. I'm saying I'm willing to accept you as you are. How much more reasonable can a man be?"

Marla closed her eyes for a moment. Her knuckles whitened as she gripped the suitcase handle more tightly. "Jack, for the last time, I'm not what you think, or what Claire would like you to believe I am. I've never been unfaithful to you. *You* were the only man I was ever 'easy' with! My biggest regret is that it's led you to think I'm that way with other men. And there's nothing between me and Rory Preston. Yes, he's been chasing me, but I've done my best to discourage him. There is no other man in my life but you!"

"All right," he said, not budging from his position in the doorway. "Then stay with me. You can't prove your innocence if you leave."

160

"Prove it!" she said, enraged. "Why should I have to prove anything to you? Why don't you and Claire prove me guilty! Why can't you just believe me?" Her voice was growing slightly hysterical now.

"God knows I want to," Jack said, his voice rising in response to hers. "But how can I?"

"Oh, this is useless! Let me by!" She pushed the end of her suitcase between him and the door frame.

He let her through, but dogged her steps as she went to the front door. "Marla, don't go!"

"Why not?" she said bitterly, never slowing her pace.

"Because . . . I love you."

She was at the door, but stopped and turned. His lean face was taut, brimming with emotion. "No, you don't," she said in a heartfelt whisper. "If you did, you'd believe me. You said it was only a sexual attraction. Maybe you were right."

He caught hold of her arms and gripped her tightly. "I didn't mean that—I was trying to hurt you. I do love you. In spite of everything, I'll always love you. I don't care what you've done. Don't leave me."

She blinked her eyes hard, her lips compressed tightly over her teeth as she tried to keep hold of her composure. He didn't believe her and never would. But he still loved her? She didn't want that kind of love.

"I'm going," she told him. "Because . . . I don't think I love you anymore." She turned quickly, broke out of his grasp and walked out the door. In moments she was inside her car, her suitcase in the backseat. As she heard him call her one last time, she drove off into the night.

Steering blindly, as if on automatic, she found herself at Ginger and Devin's house at Double Bluff a half-hour later. After sitting in her parked car for several minutes collecting herself emotionally, she got out and rang their doorbell.

161

"You think Claire is to blame?" Ginger asked later, as she and Devin sat with Marla in the comfortable atmosphere of their living room. Marla had told them the whole story.

"Claire didn't help," Marla said sadly. "But the main problem is Jack. He's always so ready to believe the worst about me. Something else could have set him off as easily as Claire's tattling. It's just no good. I should have let things be when we broke up the first time. I should have realized he would always be suspicious. Even on our honeymoon he thought I was flirting with the tour guide at Butchart Gardens—a young college kid! The only way he'd trust me is if I dressed in a nun's habit, blackened my teeth and never left the house."

"That doesn't sound like much fun," Devin said dryly.

"What will you do?" Ginger asked. "Do you need a place to stay? You can stay with us."

"I don't want to impose," Marla said. "I thought I'd go up to Oak Harbor and find a motel. I just stopped in to have someone to talk to."

"Don't be silly. Stay with us until you decide what to do. Too bad your old house is sold."

Marla smiled ironically. "Yes, I was relieved when it sold so quickly. Now I wish I had it back. It was a nice little house. I was happy enough there." Her eyes glazed with moisture. "I guess being single *was* best for me."

Ginger and Devin looked down at the carpet, apparently not knowing what to say. Marla felt self-conscious suddenly, realizing she was putting a damper on their evening. "How's the baby?" she asked Ginger, forcing a little smile. "You're not showing yet, are you? Do you have much morning sickness?"

Ginger and Devin both brightened and spent the next half-hour telling her more details about pregnancy than Marla ever wanted to know. But she was glad that they, at least, were happy and looking forward to the future. At the moment Marla thought her own future looked pretty bleak.

Jack drifted aimlessly about the house for an hour or so after Marla drove off, feeling lost, lonely and dejected. He worried about Marla. *Where had she gone? Would she be all right?*

Finally he sat down on the living room couch, elbows on his knees, and pressed his face into the palms of his hands. She was gone, and it was all his fault. He shouldn't have said some of the things he had. Instead of pointing out her weaknesses and defects, he should have emphasized that he was willing to be patient and work things out. It was what he had decided to do after he had recovered from Claire's devastating news about Marla and Preston. After working through his anguish, Jack had realized that he didn't want to live without her, even if she was unfaithful.

Why did he have to carry on and voice all his resentment about her behavior? He should have pretended to believe her and insisted on seeing a marriage counselor. A little more tact would have saved him from this.

But then—the last thing she had said was that she no longer loved him. Jack's shoulders sagged. He bent his head and pushed his fingers back through the wispy gray streaks of his blond hair. Oh, God, it *was* over.

CHAPTER NINE

Warm sunlight gradually stretched across Jack's sleeping form the next morning. It streamed from the curtained front windows to the couch where he had fallen asleep sometime in the early-morning hours. He awoke to find himself alone in the quiet house, except for Max, who was snoozing on Jack's stomach. Jack tried to sit up, but the cat wouldn't budge. Finally he picked up the animal and put it on the floor, where Max promptly yawned and stretched.

Jack put his long legs over the edge of the couch then and sat up. He rubbed his eyes as memories of the night before came clearer and clearer to his groggy brain. Combing his fingers through his mussed hair, he looked around the room. Everything was still and silent except for Max, who was licking his paw. To Jack it seemed almost as though some-one had died there.

Marla—where was she? Would she really stay away? He had to try to find her, at least to see that she was all right. More than that, he had to convince her to come back. Maybe after spending a night alone she'd be willing to recon-sider.

He looked at his watch. It was eight-thirty already. He'd slept much later than usual because he had been up so late worrying. She might even be at her office by now. Leaning toward the edge of the couch, he picked up the phone on the end table. As he dialed, he prayed it would be Marla who answered.

"Hello? Who's this? Oh, Maggie. Is Marla there?"

"Marla hasn't come in yet," Maggie said. "I'm the only one here so far. How long ago did she leave?"

"She . . . I don't know," Jack said, heat rising to his face. "I'll catch her later," he said and hung up.

Where was she? She was usually on time in the morning. One thing she prided herself on was promptness. He wondered if she might have contacted Ginger. He picked up the phone again and dialed.

"Ginger?"

"Hello, Jack." She seemed to know immediately that it was he, and he sensed the coolness in her voice. Marla must have talked to her.

"Have you seen Marla?"

"Yes. She stayed here last night. She just left for work about two minutes ago."

"Oh," Jack said, relieved to have tracked down his wife. "I—suppose she told you about . . ."

"Yes, she did." Ginger paused a moment. "She and I are best friends, and it's natural for me to be on her side, but I think you've been awfully unfair to her."

She sounded angry. Jack sank back onto the couch as he held the phone to his ear. "Why? What did she say?" he asked quietly.

"That you accused her of being untrue and chasing men, especially this Rory Preston character."

"I didn't accuse her without reason, Ginger."

"Because someone saw Preston kiss her?" Ginger's tone was impatient. "Your wife manages to fight off this lecherous man all by herself, and all you can do can is accuse her of leading him on—just because some woman you know portrayed the incident in a way that suited her own purposes?"

Jack straightened from his slouch. "But, Ginger, I know from experience that Marla can give a man a good come-on when she wants to."

"That doesn't mean she gave Preston a come-on," Ginger said, holding her ground. "She can't stand him. She said so."

"Then why did he kiss her?" Jack said, trying to make Ginger see the logic behind his thinking.

Ginger was silent for an instant. "Because he was trying to make time with her, I suppose. Why ask me? Why did Devin pick up with that girl in Chicago years ago? I'll never understand the answer to that either, even though it broke us up for years. How should *I* know why you men do the things you do? *You* ought to be able to explain Preston's actions better than me!"

Ginger was such a gentle woman, it surprised Jack to hear the nettled tone in her voice. "Well, I figure he kissed her because she asked him to, one way or another. She's good with body language."

He heard Ginger sigh with exasperation. "Jack, she can't stand the man. Why would she have wanted him to kiss her? You should have heard her describing him to us last night. It would have been funny if it wasn't so sad!"

Jack shifted in his seat. "Ginger, try to remember it's natural for her to want to make herself look innocent in your eyes."

"You're saying she was lying?"

Jack didn't answer. He didn't want to get into a fight with Ginger, too. Besides, he wasn't quite so sure he was right anymore.

"I've known Marla for years," Ginger said, "and if she's anything, she's truthful—even to the point of telling me she was attracted to Devin."

Jack raised his eyebrows, ready to seize the issue. "Exactly my point: She was interested in Devin when she was having an affair with me! She never told *me* about Devin. I found that out from you!"

Ginger was quiet for a second or two. "Maybe because there was nothing going on between him and her. She was in love with you. Love was new to her, and she got emotionally

166

mixed up for a while. Sometimes I think she showed some interest in Devin mainly to make me jealous, so I would realize I wanted him back. She told me from the first that I should remarry him. You shouldn't be so hung up about her and Devin. I'm not. Her pursuit was so restrained and short-lived, Devin never even noticed it! It's not fair to label her a flirt because of that one incident."

Jack ruminated for a long moment. Ginger's reasoning seemed to have a lot of sense, he had to admit. "What did she say about Preston?" he asked at last.

Ginger chuckled a bit. "She said his brain was in his pants."

"Anything else?"

"Yes." Ginger's tone grew serious. "She said he was getting more and more out of hand. Maggie—her co-worker—told her she shouldn't go out alone with him again to the vacant house he's been looking at. Marla laughed it off, but it sounded like Maggie was getting worried about her. Frankly, I am, too, though Marla said she had verbally ripped him apart the last time she saw him, and she didn't think he'd come back again."

"Oh?" Jack said, surprised. He hadn't heard all the details before. Because he hadn't listened, he reminded himself ruefully.

"Talk to Maggie," Ginger said. "I gather she's observed the whole situation firsthand."

"I suppose I should," Jack said, sighing. It seemed he might be wrong—again. "Well, thanks for talking to me, Ginger."

"Before you hang up, Jack, let me tell you that Marla loves you. She really does!"

Jack's expression grew forlorn. "She said she doesn't love me anymore."

"What?"

"She said it just before she left. Then she walked out with her bag packed—for good, I'm afraid."

"She didn't tell us she didn't love you," Ginger said. "I got the impression she was pretty miserable. She said she left because she couldn't live with your jealousy, but she never even hinted that she didn't love you anymore."

"No?" Jack felt like he was grabbing at straws for reassurance.

"Sometimes people say things in the heat of the moment that they don't mean. Do you want her back?"

"Of course I do."

"Then I'm sure if you just ask her—nicely—she'll come home to you."

"Really?" he said, afraid to trust Ginger's rosy view of the situation.

"Really, Jack. She'll be at work in a few minutes. Call her."

Jack spent the next ten minutes mentally rehearsing what he would say to Marla. Then he got so nervous he had to spend another ten calming himself down. At last he picked up the telephone again and dialed. As he did so, Max jumped up on the arm of the couch and began batting a paw at the wiggling telephone cord.

"Shoo! Get out of here," he said, pushing the cat away.

The secretary answered the phone this time. He asked for Marla.

"Marla Whiting."

Jack froze for an instant when he heard her voice. "It's me."

"Oh."

"I—was hoping we could talk things over."

"Not now. I'm at work," she said coolly.

"No, I meant tonight. Will you come home tonight, so we can talk?"

"Why do you want to talk, Jack? What can you have to say to a fallen woman like me?" she said in a quietly vindictive tone.

"Marla . . . I'm sorry. I—can't we see each other? It's

no good getting into it on the phone like this, with your office staff there to overhear everything."

"I agree."

"Well, how about coming home tonight?"

"No."

"Why not?"

"It's your house. I'd rather we met on neutral ground."

"It's not my house, it's ours," he said, annoyed. This certainly wasn't as easy as Ginger had seemed to think it would be. Marla sounded as if she were planning battle strategies against him.

"It was your home for years. I didn't live there long enough to consider it mine," she said.

"All right, then why don't we go out to eat?" Max jumped up on the arm of the couch again and began to bite the telephone cord. Jack tried to stop him, and the cat nipped his finger. "Ouch," he said under his breath.

"I don't think I care to be called derogatory names in a public place," Marla said.

"Marla, I wouldn't—ouch! Get out of here!" Jack swatted the cat off the couch again.

"What?"

"Max was biting the telephone wire. I chased him off."

"Don't you hurt him!"

"I didn't hurt him. I'm trying to save him from being electrocuted! If you had to walk out on me, you could have at least taken your cat." Jack immediately regretted his retort. It was just that he had a hard enough time talking to Marla without having to deal with a pesky cat, too.

"I'll come and pick him up when I have a place of my own again," she said. "Did you feed him and put fresh water in his bowl?"

"No," Jack said, his hopes sinking because she sounded like she meant to stay away permanently. "I don't know where his food is."

"Of course you do. You've seen me feed him often enough." She sounded irritable.

"I never paid attention," he said absently. Then he realized the turn their conversation was taking and a sly glimmer came into his eyes.

"It's in the cabinet under the sink," she told him. "His bowl is probably empty. You'd better put more in."

"How much?" His tone implied helpless ignorance.

"It's dry food," she said impatiently. "You just fill the bowl."

"Okay, I'll look for it—if I think of it."

"You'd better think of it!"

"I don't spend much time in the kitchen," he pointed out. "I'll be leaving for the gallery pretty soon. I may not have a chance anyway."

"It only takes a minute!"

"Maybe you'd better come over and feed him yourself," he suggested.

She was silent for several seconds. "You're not going to use my cat as bait to get me over there."

"Gee, I guess he'll starve then."

"If anything happens to that cat . . ."

"Marla, why are we talking about the cat? I want to talk about us!"

"I don't see what there is to talk about."

"I love you, and I want you to come back."

"I have no intention of coming back," she said. "I'd rather be single than go through the same old arguments with you over and over."

Her cutting words crushed him. But he realized that something in her tone and manner reminded him of himself. He remembered the hard-boiled front and tough words he had used when she was actively trying to win him back. The memory gave him a new burst of hope—maybe she was doing the same thing. "You're just saying that!" he told her,

170

putting confidence in his voice. "Underneath, I bet you missed me last night, the way I missed you."

He noticed a hesitation before she answered. "You'd lose the bet," she said.

"No, I wouldn't."

"Jack, I have work to do," she said, suddenly very much in a hurry.

"I'll let you go as soon as you agree to talk to me tonight," he pressed her.

"I don't have to agree to anything." Her voice was obstinate now.

"All right," he said with patient resolve. "I'll call you again later. Maybe you'll be more agreeable after thinking it over."

"I have had enough with you, Jack! I don't want to talk to you—I have nothing to say to you. The best thing is for both of us to get a lawyer."

Jack's body grew rigid. "No way, Marla."

"It's the only sensible thing to do," she insisted.

"I don't think it makes any sense at all."

"Well, I'm getting a lawyer. You can do as you please," she said, sighing distractedly as though at her wit's end trying to argue with him. "Good-bye."

"Marla," he cut in quickly before she hung up, "let me make one thing clear to you. I'm going to fight for our marriage. I refuse to let you go. You'll be hearing from me a lot, whether you like it or not. Meanwhile, until you come home, I'll do what I can for your cat." He hung up then without waiting for her reply. But he felt so good about the stance he had just taken that for the first time in two days he grinned.

Marla looked confused as she hung up the phone. She leaned back slightly in her swivel chair. There was something familiar . . . A light came into her eyes. It was exactly what she had said to Jack months ago. She could hear her own words: *I refuse to let you go.* Now the tables were

171

turned, and he had made her the same promise. She felt excited all at once, even a little thrilled. He wasn't going to let her go? She was eager to see how he would try to stop her. He really did love her, didn't he? she thought, her eyes misting a bit. But was he worth all the jealousy and suspicion and accusations she had to endure from him? That was the question. If she did go back to him, it would certainly be worthwhile to make him suffer a little first.

If she did go back. She replayed her own thought through her head. Had she already decided? Was she so weak in her resolution? It appeared she wasn't as tough as she liked to think—she never had been when it came to Jack. The image of his tall, rangy frame came to her mind—the blond hair, the clear blue eyes, the mustache that always needed clipping. She loved every lean, jealous bone in his body. Yes, she supposed in the end she'd go back to him. Just the thought of sleeping with him again would make her come running.

But there must be something she could do to make him see her as a trustworthy wife. His attitude toward her would have to change, otherwise how long would any reconciliation between them last? The next time she was even in the same room with another man, Jack would become suspicious again. She didn't intend to put up with that anymore. But what could she do? He wasn't a computer that she could program differently. How does a woman convince such a hard-headed man?

At about eleven-fifteen Rory Preston showed up at her office—without calling first, as had become his habit. He seemed to like to take her by surprise.

He was more tediously macho in his appearance than ever. The gold chain at his neck looked shiny in contrast to the black chest hair exposed by his half-unbuttoned shirt. He was wearing his leather jacket again, lending him an extra measure of calculated toughness. Last, but far from least, he wore very tightfitted, expensive blue jeans that not only looked ready to burst under the stress of his muscled thighs but also seemed designed to emphasize that part of his anatomy he was clearly most proud of. Obviously he had set out to impress someone. It revolted Marla to know it was her.

"Hi, Marla," he said, walking up to her desk with a cool swagger. He nodded at Maggie, who was at her desk behind Marla's. "I'd like to take one last look at that house before I make an offer."

"All right," Marla said, not at all enthused.

"What house is that?" Maggie asked.

"The one up by North Bluff," Marla said.

"You know, I need to go up there to preview it for one of my clients. Do you mind if I ride with you?"

Marla kept her face expressionless, but she wanted to smile. She knew Maggie was fibbing about needing to look at the house. "Sure you can," she told Maggie.

Preston looked very annoyed. "If I'm going to buy it, there's no use in you checking it out for someone else," he told Maggie.

"Well, you aren't sure you're going to make an offer," Marla said. "We have to keep marketing the property. We can't stop everything waiting for you."

"I'm sure I'll buy it," Preston said. "I just want one last look, that's all."

"You never know," Maggie said. "I've had lots of buyers change their minds at the last minute. I won't be in your way."

Preston was peeved, like an overgrown brat.

"Let's go then," Marla said brightly. She was very happy with Maggie's quick thinking in inviting herself along.

But Preston seemed suspicious as he accompanied the women outside to Marla's car. She sensed he was catching on to their game. Too bad, she thought blithely.

"There she is. Maggie!"

Marla and the others turned to see a middle-aged couple hurrying toward them from their car parked across the street. It was a couple Maggie had been working with. Marla glanced at her co-worker and saw her hesitant expression.

"Hello," Maggie said, stepping toward them a bit.

"We were out driving and we saw a house for sale that looks beautiful. It's near Clinton. We'd like to know the asking price. Can you show the house to us?"

"Well . . . sure," Maggie said. Marla could sense her dilemma.

"They look anxious. You'd better go with them," Marla told her.

"But . . ." Maggie's eyes were uneasy.

"See you later," Marla said congenially, opening her car door. Preston, smiling now, got in on the other side. *Darn,* Marla thought. It was extraordinarily loyal of Maggie to want to come with her and help keep Preston in line, but Marla didn't want Maggie to ruin her chance of making a sale. She'd been working with the couple for some time. Well, if fate dictated that Marla would have to go out to the house alone with Preston, then so be it. She could handle him, she assured herself.

But as she drove, her nerves grew more and more on edge. She could sense him eyeing her often, and she was glad she had worn her brown suit. The jacket covered her breasts well if she kept it buttoned over her high-collared beige blouse. Unfortunately, she realized as she happened to glance down, the front slit of the straight skirt revealed quite a bit of her leg as she sat with her foot on the gas pedal. So that was what Preston was eyeing. She tried to shift the material to cover her knees better.

"Oh, don't fix it," Preston said suggestively. "I like the view."

Marla bit back a retort and continued to tug the material over her exposed thigh. As soon as she had accomplished the task, Preston reached over and pulled the edge of the skirt back again.

"Stop it!" she said.

"Stop?" He chuckled. "Honey, I'm only warming up! To-day you're going to find out just what you've been missing."

Jack walked into Marla's office. He was a little deflated because he didn't see her car out front. A glance around the office only confirmed the fact that she wasn't in. He had decided to come and see her in person, to try to get her to have lunch with him if he could.

"Jack?"

He turned to find it was Maggie calling him. She was talking to a middle-aged man and woman at her desk. He'd overheard them discussing some house near Clinton when he came in. "Hi, Maggie," he said. He'd met her a few times since marrying Marla. "Is my wife out?"

"Yes." She turned to the couple. "Would you excuse me for just a second?" She walked around her desk to Jack and took him aside. "I'm glad you came in. Marla's out showing a vacant house to Rory Preston. Has she mentioned him to you?"

"I've heard about him."

"Did she tell you all the trouble she's having with him? That man is a first-class wolf! I'm concerned about her being alone with him in that empty house, without a phone. I was going to go with them, but then these people came and I couldn't. I think you ought to go up there and make sure she's all right."

"What's the address of this place?" Jack asked, growing worried.

In minutes Jack was on the road, driving fast toward North Bluff. The concern in Maggie's eyes was enough to convince him that Marla might actually be in some danger.

It seemed to take forever, but finally he pulled into the driveway of the vacant wood-frame house. He hurried to the front door and found it slightly ajar. He quietly pushed it open; he wanted to see what the situation was, if he could, before he made his presence known. The door opened into

175

the empty living room. When he walked in, he could hear voices coming from upstairs. Moving to the staircase, he climbed it silently.

"Come on, Marla, don't act like such a prude. You know how to have fun."

"Take your hands off me!"

"What are you going to do, scream? No one will hear you."

"I'm warning you!"

Jack rushed to the open door where the voices were coming from. He saw Rory Preston gripping Marla by her arms and leaning forward to kiss her. Arching her neck, Marla was trying to escape his mouth.

"Come on, baby, let's cooperate," Preston said, his manner growing rough. "I like spitfires, but—"

Anger and adrenaline fired Jack for action. He was about to race in when, to his astonishment, he saw Marla give the man a sharp knee kick to the groin. It almost hurt Jack to watch it. Preston immediately doubled over in pain. Marla's eyes burned bright with vindication and feminine contempt. Turning quickly, she began marching at a fast clip toward the door when she saw Jack. She was breathing hard and appeared startled at the sight of her husband.

"What are you doing here?" she said, anger still in her voice.

Jack couldn't help it—he backed away from her slightly, fearing he might be in for the same as Preston had gotten. "I'm—here to rescue you," he said.

She stared at him as if perplexed for a moment, then looked relieved and smiled. Hurrying up to him, she put her hands on his chest. "You are?"

"Looks like you don't need a hero, though," he said, laughing. He glanced over at Preston, who was only now recovering from her blow.

"You bitch!" Preston blustered, standing up unsteadily and glaring at Marla.

176

Jack's smile died, and he felt a rush of rage. Putting Marla aside, he strode to Preston and grabbed the man roughly by the lapels of his leather jacket. Rory Preston was muscular, but Jack was taller. He peered down at Preston from his superior height as if the other man were a bug.

"No one calls my wife names!" he rasped. "You got what you asked for. I can punch a lot harder than she can kick, so unless you want more of the same, I'd get the hell out of here!"

His face soured with humiliation, Preston backed away and hurried past Marla out the door. Jack joined her in the doorway and watched Preston bound unsteadily down the steps, obviously still hurting. Jack couldn't help but chuckle when he noticed the man's pants had split at the back seam, allowing his white briefs to peak through. His tight jeans had apparently ripped when he'd bent over suddenly from Marla's blow.

Preston went to the front door, then stopped short and turned around. "Hey, I came in your car. How do I get back?"

"That's only one of your problems, pal," Jack said, much amused. "Your pants are ripped."

Preston grabbed at the seat of his designer jeans. His face flushed a deep red. Jack almost felt sorry for him. He had lost both Marla and his pride in one excruciating moment.

Jack escorted Marla down the steps. "All right," he said, "I'll drive you back to Langley. Marla, you follow us in your car."

The drive back to the office was uneventful. Preston, morose, said nothing. When Jack pulled up in front of Marla's office, he stopped the car and both men got out. Marla pulled up behind in her car.

On the sidewalk Jack turned to Preston, took hold of one of his lapels and said in quiet warning, "I'm going to tell Marla to call the police if she ever finds you hanging around.

And if I ever catch you bothering her again, you'll be a lot worse off than you are today. You got me?"

Preston nodded belligerently and walked up the street to his car. Marla came up to Jack then and took his arm. "Is everything okay? What did you say to him?" She appeared worried, even upset.

"I just told him not to show his face around here again." He looked at her with concern. "Are you all right? You seem a little shook up."

"I was nervous driving behind you in the car—afraid you might get into a fight with him." She brushed some wind-blown hair out of her eyes. Jack could see her fingers shaking.

"He didn't say boo," Jack assured her. "He's one of those men who's all show and no guts. Looks like he scared you, though." He put his arm around her shoulders. "You didn't look frightened when you kneed him in the groin."

"I was angry then," she said, leaning against him. "I guess now I'm beginning to realize what happened. I never had to fight off a man before. At least not like that."

"You were pretty impressive!" he told her, giving her an extra hug. Her slender body felt frail and vulnerable against his. "But maybe you'd better take the rest of the day off. I'll drive you home."

Marla nodded, and Jack was relieved that she didn't object to coming home with him. He waited a few minutes while she stopped in at the office to tell the secretary she wouldn't be in for the rest of the day. Maggie was gone, but Jack made a mental note to thank her for telling him Marla's whereabouts.

He also ought to thank her for giving him the opportunity to see how trustworthy his wife was, he thought, feeling guilty. In the future he wouldn't be nearly so quick to doubt her.

"Are you hungry? Want to stop for lunch somewhere?" he asked Marla when they got into his car.

She glanced at her watch. "I'm not very hungry, but I suppose we should eat. It's almost one."

"How about the little place near the movie theater?"

She agreed. It was only a couple of blocks away on First Street, but they drove anyway. After they had found a table and ordered sandwiches, Jack said, "I'm proud of you, the way you handled that guy. I'll be more careful about getting on your bad side in the future," he said with a smile. He was trying to buck her up with humor. She still seemed to be suffering some nervous aftereffects from her encounter with Preston. Her movements were too quick, and she seemed disquieted.

"Are you kidding?" she said with a slight smile that wasn't reflected in her eyes. "You scared *me* the way you grabbed him and yelled at him there at the house. I don't think I ever saw you dangerous before."

Her words gave Jack's ego a boost. He wanted his wife to admire him. He thought of joking, in a sexy way, that he was always dangerous, but thought better of it. She was too shaken to start any verbal foreplay. He supposed it must be upsetting to a woman to have to fight off a man much bigger and stronger than she was. In fact, the more he thought about it, the more he wondered how devastating the mental effect on her might be. If she hadn't done what she did, and if Maggie hadn't told him to go after her, who knew what might have happened?

The thought unsettled Jack for a moment, but he forced himself not to dwell on it for her sake. The incident was over. He needed to calm her down and give her support.

"I'm just a pussycat around you," he joked, hoping to dispel the idea of danger that seemed fixed in her thoughts.

Marla's expression changed. "How's Maxie?"

Jack's shoulders slumped a bit. He'd said the wrong word. "He's fine."

"Did you feed him?"

"Yes, and I gave him fresh water. When I left, he was

shredding the roll of paper towels on the sink, so he's in good form."

Marla smiled then. A little sheepishly, Jack thought. "Thanks," she said.

"Does this mean we can be friends again?" he asked, his voice suddenly a little strained with anxiety.

"Friends?" Her brows drew together.

"Are you going to come home?"

She looked down, then grinned. "I guess so."

"I'm sorry, Marla, that I ever doubted you. I'm sorry it took all this to convince me."

She shrugged, almost shy in her manner. It was unusual for Marla. "It's flattering to have a husband who'll rough up any man who comes near me," she said. "It's nice to feel protected for a change. I've always taken care of myself. Though I'm glad I can, it's reassuring to know that you'd run to my rescue like you did." There were unshed tears shining in her eyes. Jack was touched. He reached across the table to hold her hand. "How did you find out where I was?" she asked.

"I came to the office to see you, and Maggie told me. She was very concerned."

"Maggie's sweet, isn't she?"

Jack nodded. "So's Ginger. I called her this morning, and she stuck up for you tooth and nail. You know how to pick your friends!"

Marla smiled. "I know how to pick a husband, too."

She seemed much calmer now, and there were lights playing in her eyes. How beautiful she was! Jack wished he could paint her now, just like this. Someday he would.

"I don't know if I'm such a good husband," he said, lowering his eyes from her lovely face. "I jump to conclusions, I'm suspicious without cause and I'm unreasonable."

"Yes, that's true," Marla said lightly, her eyes glimmering with fun. It was beginning to excite him. "But you have your good points, too."

180

"Like what?"

"Oh . . . you're handsome, you're talented and intelligent, sensitive and . . . well, the other traits I can't mention in a restaurant." She looked down at her place mat innocently.

Jack wasn't entirely sure she meant what he thought she meant. After all, she was upset, and he didn't think she'd really be in a mood to think about . . .

The waitress brought their sandwiches and set them in front of Jack and Marla. They ate in silence for a while until Jack thought of something he wanted to tell her.

"Don't you think you ought to quit real estate pretty soon?" he asked gently. "Especially after what happened today?"

Her dark eyes grew a little troubled. "I would, but I haven't figured out what else to do instead."

"Why don't you run my art gallery for me?"

She looked up from her sandwich, her eyes widening. "You want me to? What about Claire?"

"I went to the gallery this morning. When she came in, I told her I didn't need her anymore."

"You did?" Marla said, setting her sandwich down. "Really?"

"Yup." He could see how pleased she was. She looked like she was ready to get up and lead a cheer.

"Was Claire upset?" Marla asked.

"She didn't seem too happy. But I think she understands why I let her go. I may have had my doubts and said some things to you I'll always regret, but I won't let anyone else malign you or spread gossip about you. Good as Claire was at her work, I just decided I didn't want her around anymore."

Marla looked gratified by what he said. "So," she said with a smile, "when do I start? What are my duties?"

"You can start tomorrow, if you like." They spent the rest of the lunch talking about her new job.

Jack drove her home then. As soon as she walked in, she found Max in the living room, picked him up and cooed to him. It was ridiculous, but sometimes Jack felt jealous of that darned cat.

"You talk to him like he was a person," he said.

She smiled as she held Max, her cheek against his furry white face. "Well, he is like a little person in a cat suit."

Jack lifted his eyes to the ceiling. "A cat suit? What kind of suit do I have to put on to get all the pampering he gets?"

"Oh, I don't know," Marla said in an enigmatic tone. "You look best in no suit at all." She set Max on the floor.

Jack looked at her twice as she stood again to face him. He wondered if she meant that as a hint. He'd love to take her to bed and make their relationship everything it was before their big fight. But he didn't think he should just yet. Women were delicate. He didn't think he should push himself on her, not when she was still recovering from being molested by another man. "You look a little tired, Marla. Maybe you should lie down and rest," he said sincerely. "You've had a rough morning."

"Are you going back to the gallery?"

"No. I'll just leave it closed until tomorrow. I don't want to leave you alone after what happened, at least not today," he said.

She walked up to him and put her arms around him. "That's so thoughtful of you, Jack. I would like to lie down. Why don't you come with me?" She gazed up into his face.

Her dark hair fell luxuriantly about her shoulders, and her brown eyes were winsome and eager. Her body was warm and slender in his arms. God, he wanted her. "But you know what would happen . . ."

"I hope so." She smiled and leaned up to kiss him lightly on the mouth.

Jack tried not to respond. "Marla, do you think we should? You just had a bad experience this morning. I think you ought to take a little time to recover. If we make love, you might remember what he tried to do and it might upset you."

Marla backed away from him slightly and looked at him as if she was a little startled. "I hadn't thought of that," she said.

"You seemed pretty shaken up after it was over," Jack reminded her.

"I was, a little," she said. "I see . . . you think it might bring on a trauma or something if we . . ."

"Well, I think it would be best if you rested for a while, darling." He looked down at her seriously. "You liked the fact that I was protective of you this morning. If I'm going to take good care of you, it may mean that I should even protect you from me sometimes."

A whimsical expression that mystified him came and went in her eyes. "You're really wonderful, Jack," she said softly. "Maybe you're right. I'll go and lie down for a while." She raised her lips to his cheek in a chaste kiss and then went into their bedroom and closed the door.

Jack stood in the middle of the living room and looked at the shut door. He felt a little off-balance somehow, but he didn't know quite why. He had done the noble thing, and she had followed his advice.

That was it. She had been much too docile about it. Marla was rarely so unquestioning about anything. She was only that agreeable about making love, not about not making love.

He eyed Max stretching out on the sofa, looking well fed and comfortable, his furry little body sleek and content— like Marla after making love. Jack sighed. He wished now she had argued with him a little more.

On the other side of the closed door, Marla was chuckling silently. *Jack is so adorable,* she thought as she opened the bottom drawer of her dresser. Most of her lingerie was at Ginger's house in the suitcase she had so hastily packed. But she was glad she had left the items she was pulling out of the drawer now.

She began to take off her suit jacket. It was kind of Jack to treat her like a fragile flower, and she appreciated it. But he ought to know by now that while she might be slender and delicate-looking, she wasn't any frail lily. Yes, she had been a little rattled about having actually kicked a man in the groin. But it made her feel good that she was able to protect herself so well.

What had really shaken her, for a little while, was Jack. She had truly been afraid he'd get into a fistfight with Preston. And while Jack was taller and probably more agile, she wasn't at all sure he would come out on top in a grapple with a man who looked like he spent all his time pumping iron when he wasn't selling cars or pursuing women. She had feared Jack might get his nose bloodied, a tooth knocked out or worse. Jack was an artist and a lover, not a fighter, and it would have killed her to see him hurt.

Well, she thought, hanging up her skirt and blouse in the closet, it all had worked out right and she had quickly calmed down. If she looked tired, it was because she hadn't slept well last night, away from Jack. But she wasn't ready for a nap, not yet.

Marla straightened her spine and sucked in her stomach as she wrapped the corset around her torso, reaching back to fasten the long series of hooks and eyes that made it fit so snugly. She hadn't worn the black-and-red garment since that night she had gone back to Jack's studio so he could finish the painting. Seducing him had been her purpose that night, and it was now, too. But she quite honestly thought the task would be a piece of cake this time.

She put on the black lace stockings and fastened them to the garters, then pulled on the wispy black panties. After finding and putting on her black high heels, she checked herself in the full-length mirror on the sliding closet door. She adjusted the lacy décolletage so that every curve was as

184

tantalizing as it could be, then looked herself over from head to foot. Her legs were long and shapely, her bare thighs accentuated by the black of the panties above and the tops of the stockings below. Her waist looked minuscule, accenting her rounded hips and trussed-up bosom. So what if she couldn't breathe? If Jack didn't succumb, there was definitely something wrong!

Her heart thumping with anticipation, she opened the door and walked into the living room. Jack was sitting on the couch at one end, reading a newspaper. Maxie was curled up on the other end, asleep.

"Jack," she called softly.

He put down the paper and looked up. His blue eyes had a startled expression for a few moments as he gazed over her, but then he slowly smiled. "I always seem to underestimate you," he said dryly. "You don't feel like following my advice about a quiet nap, I take it."

"No," she said, walking smoothly toward him with swaying, feminine strides. He stood up as she approached and put his hands at her waist. "I'm in the mood for something else."

"And just what is that?" he said as he eyed the creamy skin that plumped invitingly above the black lace bodice. Already she could sense his breath quickening.

"Making love?" Her eyes probed his longingly, wanting his approval for her idea.

He raised his blond-brown eyebrows in mock admonition, his eyes playful. "You're sure you're up for it? Let me warn you: You're asking for it in this little outfit! I can still feel my frustration from the last time you wore it—all to get me to marry you! Minx!"

Marla grinned and pressed herself against him. Indeed, she could feel his frustration quite clearly as her thighs met his. It made her pulse race. He was all but seduced already, she thought with satisfaction. "What am I asking for?" she said, her eyes all wide innocence.

Jack chuckled warmly in his throat. "You're something else! It's no wonder I worry about you and other men."

Marla dropped her eyes sadly. It wasn't what she wanted to hear.

"I didn't mean to bring that up," he quickly apologized. He drew her closer in a strong, anxious hug. "I can't help but be possessive and wary. You're so desirable, so unbelievably sexy. And you enjoy sex so much! You're exactly what every man dreams of."

Locked in his loving embrace, Marla couldn't help but forgive him and smile as her cheek pressed into his shoulder. She was happy she could fulfill her husband's dreams. "I always heard a man wanted a woman who could cook," she said, looking up at him, her eyes dancing.

Jack laughed, gazing down at her fondly. "Who needs to eat?" he said tenderly. "I only need to love you."

Her eyes misted. She slipped her arms around his neck and kissed him. He caught her up tightly to him and returned her kiss hotly, his lips firm and eager on hers. His hands moved downward from her waist over the lacy edge of the corset to the filmy panties covering her derriere. She felt his fingers slip beneath the material to squeeze and caress her flesh. The sensation made her giggle with delight even as it aroused her more.

Jack drew his mouth away and smiled at her reaction. "You're fun to make love to," he said.

She smiled, but a cloud passed over her eyes as she remembered something. "Last time," she began hesitantly, "when it was so wonderful . . . you said you hadn't been making love, that you were just trying to satisfy me. Did you say that out of anger? Or—did you mean it?"

Jack slowly looked down, his eyes penitent. "I'm afraid what I said was true. I thought you were involved with Preston because of what Claire told me. I was jealous, of course, and hurt. I thought if I wore you out in bed, you wouldn't go back to him. But, somehow, it turned into an incredible experience for both of us. I'm sorry about my original intention, but I can't regret what happened." He looked at her, his eyes imploring her understanding and forgiveness.

Marla's face gradually broke into a grin. "So you tried to love the daylights out of me! Well, you succeeded." Her dark eyes glowed with desire. "Now you've spoiled me," she said, her voice lowering to a heady whisper. "After that night I could never be content with any man but you. I want you to love me that way again, Jack . . . now . . . long, and hard and relentless . . . until I'm limp. The way only you can do it. Please, darling?"

The expression in Jack's eyes was touching and awesome as he gazed down at her. He looked like he wanted to weep and devour her all at once. In compromise, he kissed her once more, sweeping her up in masterful arms that squeezed the breath out of her but left her delirious with joy. An instant later he was lowering her to the couch. Vaguely she noticed Maxie jump out of the way as she lay back and opened her arms to Jack. In moments impeding clothing was pushed aside and Jack was within her, strong and masculine, filling her with love, fulfilling her need, on his way to quenching her desire while she responded with kisses and caresses to pleasure him in return. She knew even then it would be a memorable afternoon. But only one of many to come.

Maxie, meanwhile, stretched and yawned on the carpeted floor, where he had jumped to get out of their way. He watched them for a minute, curious at all the writhing and deep breathing, then yawned again. They were always doing that. A cat couldn't get a decent snooze anymore. Maybe he'd go into the kitchen and see if he could find some paper to shred.

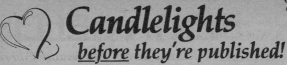

MARIANNE HARVEY

Know the passions and perils, the love and the lust, as the best of the past is reborn in her books.

____THE DARK HORSEMAN	11758-5-44	$3.50
____GYPSY FIRES*	12860-9-13	2.95
____GYPSY LEGACY*	12990-7-16	2.95
____STORMSWEPT*	19030-4-13	3.50

*Writing as Mary Williams

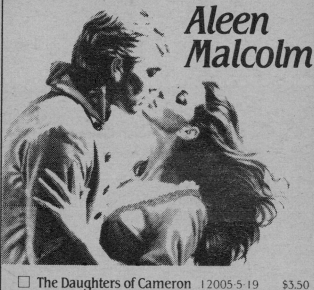

All-new **Candlelight Newsletter**

An exceptional, *free* offer awaits readers of Dell's incomparable Candlelight Ecstasy and Supreme Romances.

Subscribe to our all-new CANDLELIGHT NEWSLETTER and you will receive—at absolutely no cost to you—exciting, exclusive information about today's finest romance novels and novelists. You'll be part of a select group to receive sneak previews of upcoming Candlelight Romances, well in advance of publication.

You'll also go behind the scenes to "meet" our Ecstasy and Supreme authors, learning firsthand where they get their ideas and how they made it to the top. News of author appearances and events will be detailed, as well. And contributions from the Candlelight editor will give you the inside scoop on how she makes her decisions about what to publish—and how *you* can try your hand at writing an Ecstasy or Supreme.

You'll find all this and more in Dell's CANDLELIGHT NEWSLETTER. And best of all, *it costs you nothing.* That's right! It's Dell's way of thanking our loyal Candlelight readers and of adding another dimension to your reading enjoyment.

Just fill out the coupon below, return it to us, and look forward to receiving the first of many CANDLELIGHT NEWSLETTERS—overflowing with the kind of excitement that only enhances our romances!

 **DELL READERS SERVICE—DEPT. BR778E
P.O. BOX 1000, PINE BROOK, N.J. 07058**

Name_____

Address_____

City_____

State_____ Zip_____